"I have no doubt you were ▮
an action hero isn't really pr ▮
ability to act."

She immediately realized that she'd said ▮
shouldn't have.

His eyes turned surprisingly sad..

Instinctively, she raced over to him, placing a hand on his shoulder. He stood slowly, the sadness in his eyes changing to pain.

They stared at each other, anticipation sizzling, and tension crackling. Then she pulled him gently to her, placing her arms around him. His head dropped to her shoulder and rested.

She raised a hand, placing it on his head as she touched him softly. His body tensed, coiled like a spring and then he sighed softly. His body relaxing as if the pain he carried had left him. Inside she moaned, his closeness stirred something inside her she'd thought long buried.

She loved the feel of his body against her own. He was all hardness and male. She ached to run her hand against his firmness, to feel his warmth beneath her palms.

At that moment, he raised his head and looked her full in the eyes, as if to question what was happening between them. But she didn't want to think logically. She just wanted to feel.

Books by Wayne Jordan

Harlequin Kimani Romance

Embracing the Moonlight
One Gentle Knight
To Love a Knight
Always a Knight
Midnight Kisses
Saved by Her Embrace
To Love You More
I'll Stand By You
Touch My Heart

WAYNE JORDAN

For as long as he can remember, Wayne Jordan has loved to read, and he also enjoyed creating his own make-believe worlds. This love for reading and writing continued, and in November 2005 his first book, Capture the Sunrise, was published by BET Books.

Wayne has always been an advocate for romance, especially African-American romance. In 1999 he founded www.romanceincolor.com, a website that focuses on African-American romance and its authors.

Wayne is a high school teacher and a graduate of the University of the West Indies. He holds a B.A. in Literature and Linguistics and a M.A. in Applied Linguistics. He lives on the beautiful tropical island of Barbados, which, with its white sands and golden sunshine, is the perfect setting for the romance stories he loves to create. Of course, he still takes time out to immerse himself in the latest release from one of his favorite authors.

Touch My Heart

WAYNE JORDAN

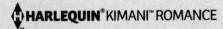

HARLEQUIN® KIMANI™ ROMANCE

This story is dedicated to The real Nugget,

who passed away earlier this year.

You were a bundle of energy and joy.

We miss you.

Recycling programs
for this product may
not exist in your area.

ISBN-13: 978-0-373-86335-8

TOUCH MY HEART

Copyright © 2013 by Wayne Jordan

For questions and comments about the quality of this book please contact us at CustomerService@Harlequin.com.

Printed in U.S.A.

www.Harlequin.com

Dear Reader,

Touch My Heart is a special milestone. It's my tenth
full-length novel. Since Capture the Sunrise debuted
in November 2005, I have continued to improve as
a writer. I always strive to create the best book, and
fortunately, readers have enjoyed my work thus far.
After a new release, I get emails from readers asking,
"When is the next one?"

I wish writing were as easy as manufacturing items on
an assembly line. With age and experience, there also
comes a better understanding and appreciation of the
writing craft, and I want my books to be even better.
However, the day job, illness and other external factors
often intrude on the writing process. Touch My Heart
was not an easy book to write. I struggled with the
plot, discarded the first draft after I realized I didn't like
most of it and started again. I could have edited and
submitted, but I wanted to create a story my readers
would love as much as I did.

This version of Touch My Heart is that story: an intense
romance about the healing power of love.

Thanks for your unwavering support.

Until next time,

Wayne Jordan

To my editor, Shannon Criss, whose patience was put to the test during the creation of this story. There were times when I felt like giving up, but your understanding gave me the courage to press on.

To my agent, Cheryl Ferguson, who has been there from the day I got "The Call." Thanks for your unwavering support. You are truly an awesome lady.

Prologue

From the single window in the room, Aaliyah watched as her eleven-year-old sister, Eboni, stepped into the white BMW. She'd wanted to run downstairs to hug Eboni one last time, but Mrs. Grice, her foster mother, had forbidden it.

A wave of sadness washed over her. Despite the fact that Eboni had finally found a family, Aaliyah was alone and it scared her. For the umpteenth time since her parents' tragic death a year earlier, she felt the familiar rush of helplessness. She wanted to cry, wanted to scream out at a world that had shattered the fairy-tale life she and her sisters had once lived.

She had prayed that each of her three sisters would find a family before she did. Because now, hopefully, her turn would come. But as she looked around at the other girls in the room, she knew that hope was a fragile thing.

Several of the girls, most of them around her age, still remained. While her younger sisters, Cindi and Keisha, who had been adopted several months ago, epitomized cuteness, and Eboni had a "good little girl" look about her, Aaliyah knew she didn't have much to offer any family. No one wanted a girl who looked way older than fourteen years.

She sighed, wondering if she would ever find happiness. Since her parents' death, things had changed. Her once carefree existence had slipped away with the words of the police officer who'd delivered the tragic news.

Now alone in the orphanage, she had to survive. At least she was glad her sisters were gone. She was strong and knew how to stand up for herself. She'd protected her sisters like a lioness would protect her offspring.

She turned toward the television. Disney's *Beauty and the Beast* had just started. She knew the story well, that Belle would find happiness and true love.

She grimaced. She wanted the same thing for herself. Maybe someday a prince would come to her rescue.

While she often feigned cynicism, inside she still believed in happily ever after.

The sky, just a moment ago vibrant with color, had slowly morphed into dull shades of gray.

Night then covered the island like a dark blanket.

Dominic raced across the wide expanse, his focus on getting away from the house and village in the distance.

He moved like the wind, his feet so familiar with the terrain that he knew exactly where the cracks were. The large colonial house where his mother had once worked loomed before him, its flickering lights guiding him. On occasion, he'd sneaked on the grounds and been awed at the opulence of the owners.

Today he did not stop, preferring to keep running until he reached the cliff face. He then immediately collapsed on the ground.

He didn't want to cry. He was fourteen and tears were for sissies, or so said the boys in the village.

He couldn't let them see him, but there should be no shame in crying at one's mother's death.

When he'd returned home from school that afternoon and gone to the kitchen, he had hoped that by some miracle she had cooked. But there was nothing.

He had peeped into his mother's room and had found her there fast asleep. Or so he'd thought until he'd stepped inside and a chill had washed over his body.

He had rushed to the bed and placed his hand against her chest to find that her heart was no longer beating.

Chapter 1

"She needs a makeover!" Cheryl observed as she inspected Aaliyah with the discerning eyes of a fashionista.

"I don't need any makeover," Aaliyah retorted, turning to face Cheryl, her sister's bubbly best friend. "I'm fine as I am!"

"I'm going to have to agree with Cheryl on this one," Eboni interjected, lowering herself onto the couch, her stomach protruding with the evidence of her seventh month of pregnancy. "We definitely need to do something about your style, or should I say lack thereof. It's almost as if you're deliberately trying to make yourself unattractive."

A wave of sadness washed over Aaliyah. She did not respond. Her sister's words were too close to the truth for comfort. Since the death of her husband, Andrew, almost three years ago, she'd tried to keep herself safe from the advances of her male colleagues. In the weeks following his death, she quickly learned that men seemed to think that widows and divorcées were easy targets.

She knew she was not bad looking, but at work she tried to play down that attractiveness, drawing attention from her natural beauty. Unfortunately, she'd allowed the frumpy look to overflow into other areas of her life. Maybe it was time to start living again. Maybe she should let Cheryl work her magic. She was on vacation anyway and wouldn't be back to work for another few weeks. When her break was over she could go back to being her prim, proper and very safe self.

"Come here," Cheryl said, pulling her toward the mirror. "Tell me what you see."

She lifted her head up and stared into the mirror. She wore no makeup now, but remembered when a touch of color and mascara would make her eyes wide and innocent. When a splash of her favorite lipstick would make her lips look soft and pouty. Her hair, thick and healthy looking, was confined to its usual bun. She cringed. She looked much older that she had three years ago. The wedding photo on the mantelpiece was clear evidence.

In the photo, she looked happy. She'd found something special on that day and it had been taken away from her too fast.

"So what do you think we should improve, Eboni?" Cheryl asked as she undid Aaliyah's bun.

Eboni cocked her head to the side and looked up at her sister. "She's beautiful even without makeup. I'd suggest we don't do anything too drastic. The foundation is good. Just a bit here and there to improve the exterior design. The woman has no sense of style whatsoever."

Aaliyah gasped. She couldn't believe they were talking about her as if she weren't standing there.

"Hello. I'm still here, you know."

"I'm sorry," Eboni apologized, laughter in her eyes, "but we are concerned for you. I know you are not totally happy."

"What do you mean?" Aaliyah asked.

"We know that you still miss Andrew. I can see it in your eyes whenever you think I'm not looking."

About to deny it, she paused. Lying to Eboni made no sense.

"Yes, I miss him. He was the love of my life. He took a broken girl without any family and taught her how to love and hope again. I won't ever find love like that again."

"You can't say that, Aaliyah," Eboni cautioned. "Maybe there is someone else out there for you. It's possible to find love again."

"Eboni, I know you've found your fairy-tale romance. I remember Mom reading those stories to us years ago, but there is fantasy and then there is reality. For a while I lived that happily ever after, but that soon came to an end. Yes, maybe I need to start living again, but I have no room in my life for love or fairy tales."

"I think you're wrong, but at least you know you need to move forward," Eboni replied.

"Well, while I like all this love talk," Cheryl injected, snorting loudly, "I think we need to get going if we want to have her transformed anytime soon."

"I'm all ready to go," Eboni said, slowly rising from the chair. "I just need to go upstairs to collect my handbag and purse. Have to make sure I have all my credit cards."

"I won't have you spending money on me. I can bring my own credit card. Andrew left me quite comfortable."

"That's fine, but let me do this," Eboni reasoned. "I haven't brought anything for you. I have years of birthday gifts to catch up on."

"Okay, but I'm still bringing mine along. I'm paying for half of whatever we buy."

"Well, since I'm not rich like you ladies, can I throw in a few outfits for myself?" Cheryl asked. "I saw this darling little dress at Macy's."

Ebony couldn't control her outburst of laughter.

"Cheryl, we know you're not deprived, but your birthday is coming up, so I'll pay for whatever you want."

"Good," Cheryl stated. "Since I'm hungry, can we do lunch first? We can spend the rest of the afternoon shopping."

"Within reason, please. Remember, I get tired easily," Eboni said.

"We know, momma-to-be," Cheryl said. "We know. Just imagine, in another two months, you'll be even more drained."

"Don't remind me. I'm looking forward to the babies, but the thought of the pain and sleepless nights scares the hell out of me."

She reached for her phone. "I'll just call Darren and let him know I'm on my way out."

Aaliyah looked at her sister and Cheryl. Despite what they were thinking, she'd changed some. Since reconciling with Eboni just over a year ago, she'd welcomed friendship with both her and Cheryl. They spent a lot of time together and of course, their girls' nights out every few weeks were welcomed.

"Okay, girls. Come, let's go," Aaliyah chirped, hoping she sounded genuine. The best thing to do would be to submit willingly and get it over. She did all she could to stifle a groan.

Dominic Wolfe limped slowly into the room. He knew what was coming, but he didn't particularly care to hear it.

He eased himself into the chair, his eyes still averted. He could almost image the look in his doctor's eyes. All he could think of was getting on the aircraft and heading back home.

He cleared his throat, willing his doctor and friend, Charles Graham, to look up. When he did, he did it slowly, glancing in Dominic's direction as if Dominic were a schoolboy about to be punished. In fact, Dominic felt like a young child under his probing gaze.

"So you've been giving trouble again." His tone was sharp.

"Don't blame me for that woman's incompetence. I should have fired her the day she arrived."

"Instead, it took you three days. A whole week longer than the last nurse."

"She was more interested in sucking up to me."

"Well, you *are* a celebrity!"

"Was! That's all in the past."

"You can regain the strength in your hand again."

"But not my leg. It's almost completely shattered. I may have to live with this limp," he grumbled.

"You saved that little girl's life."

"I know, but it doesn't stop me from being bitter at the world. I've earned the right to be." His honesty startled him.

"So what do you plan on doing?" Charles asked. "You need the therapy."

"I plan on leaving New York and visiting the island."

"Barbados?" Charles could not keep the surprise out of his voice. "You haven't visited the island in ages."

"I have a home there. I've been there weekends when I've wanted to get away."

"You have? You could have told me. I was under the impression that you didn't have any family there."

Dominic shrugged. "No, there is no one there. A few years ago, I was browsing through a real estate website and saw the house available. It's close to the village where I once lived."

"Going there may be a good thing. Maybe the fresh ocean breeze will help you to recover. However…"

"However, what?"

"I'm going to insist that for at least six months, you have a therapist. I know the perfect person. I know a nurse who completed her certification in physiotherapy a few months ago. She may only have a few months' experience, but she's good. I've seen her work with some of the kids in pediatrics."

"So…I'm a kid now," Dominic growled.

"Sometimes." Charles threw back his head and laughed out loud.

Dominic glared at him.

"All joking aside…" Charles responded. His brow creased with worry. "I'm serious about the young lady coming to work with you. As long as she agrees."

"So I have no choice in the matter?" he mumbled.

"You do have a choice," Charles stated firmly. "But I'm sure you will agree with me when I tell you that you either comply to further therapy or your leg is going to get worse. You can be as stubborn as you want to be, but that's your reality," Charles snapped. "You make the choice. It's your damn leg."

"Are doctors supposed to talk to their patients like that?" Dominic challenged.

"I'm not just any doctor. I'm your doctor and I can talk to you any way I want. I've reached the stage when I'm tired of your childish behavior. So what if you've lost your career. Is that the measure you take to define yourself? The fact that your celebrity status is no more? When we were at school together, I admired your drive and determination. I knew you wanted more for yourself. I didn't realize that what you wanted had nothing to do with your talent, but how people see you and the number of groupies you could bed. That's not the man who was my best friend. You were a fighter then. What I see now is just a pale imitation of the man you wanted to be." Charles stared at him, his nostrils flaring with anger.

Dominic could feel the color drain from his face. He stood abruptly, knocking the cane down and stumbling. His leg flamed with pain and he fell to the floor. He lay still, feeling angry rather than embarrassed.

Footsteps sounded. He looked up and Charles looked down, his face unsmiling, unsympathetic. He shook his head slowly.

"I'm going to go get lunch. You can get yourself up since you seem to want to be helpless down there. I'll get Janice to come in a moment. You can tell her what you want to do. She'll tell me your decision."

With that, Charles walked out the room without a backward glance.

Inside, fury surged. Words he hadn't used for ages slipped from between his lips and sounded strange. His mother would have been shocked to hear them.

He raised himself slowly, his weight on one arm. He then tumbled awkwardly into the chair.

For a while he sat there. He couldn't believe that Charles had walked out, but by the time Janice walked into the office, he realized how silly he had been.

"You can let Charles know he can start making the arrangements," he said calmly. "I leave for Barbados tomorrow."

The phone produced its usual musical interlude. Aaliyah groaned, burrowing herself deeper into the covers, willing the sound to stop. She sighed in contentment when it did. The long afternoon had finally taken its toll on her body; her feet felt as if they would fall off. She grunted when the ringing started again.

She stretched a hand out and, with unexpected precision, grasped the retro phone, pulling it quickly to her ear.

"Hello," she greeted.

"Good evening, Aaliyah. It's Dr. Graham."

She sat up, immediately wondering if something was wrong with one of her patients. "Good evening, Dr. Graham. How can I help you?"

She'd only started working with him a few months ago in the physiotherapy department. He was a brilliant surgeon and she'd been delighted about the opportunity to learn from him.

"I'm calling you with a little proposal."

"Proposal?"

"How'd you like to go work in Barbados for a few months?"

"Barbados?"

"I have a client who needs a physiotherapist to work with him for the next few months. Would you be interested?"

"How long do I have to think about it?" she asked.

"I'll need an answer in the morning, in case I have to look for someone else. You don't have to worry about your job here. I'll make arrangements for your leave. When it's over you can return to your current position. You're the first person I thought about for this job. You've been doing great work. This would be good training."

"I'll definitely think about it. When would I be expected to start?"

"You'd be leaving a week from today."

"That soon?"

"Yes, that soon. Just think about it overnight. You'd of course be compensated very well."

"How well?" she asked out of pure curiosity.

When she heard Doctor Graham state the figure, she almost fainted.

"You're sure that is what's being offered each month?"

He laughed. "Yes, Aaliyah. For as long as my client needs the treatment. He definitely needs the help. I'm worried about him. He's already gotten rid of two therapists."

"And you think I can handle him?"

"I know you can handle him. He needs a gentle hand but lots of firmness."

"I promise I'll consider it. Can I call you in the morning?"

"I was hoping I didn't have to wait so long, but I'll try to be patient."

"Good night, then, Doctor Graham. I'll speak with you soon."

"You have a good night, Aaliyah."

After the phone disconnected, she continued to stare at the handset before she eventually put it down, pulling the covers back over her.

She didn't need to think. Before she'd put her phone down, she'd made her decision. Too many life changes had happened today. It was almost as if fate were intervening.

She would go. She had to go. She needed a change, just as Eboni had said that afternoon. She wondered if the change of surroundings would heal her of the ache she felt each night as she lay in bed alone. She missed Andrew. Sometimes in the stillness of the night, the familiar hint of the Irish Spring soap he used wafted through the air.

She rose again, picked up the phone and dialed Eboni's number to share her plans.

Chapter 2

One week later, Aaliyah looked out the cab window as miles and miles of sugar-cane fields flashed by. Barbados was spectacular. She'd seen advertisements on television, but nothing had prepared her for the reality of the island's beauty. On her way from the airport, she'd passed gated communities with massive contemporary houses. But she'd also seen quaint chattel houses nestled among the cane fields.

It was early afternoon, and as the car sped along the highway, a cool breeze gently caressed her face. She realized that nature knew how to provide relief for the scorching tropical heat.

"We don't have much farther to go," Desmond, the driver told her. She loved his accent, tinged with the warmth of the tropic sun. "I know you must be tired and hungry. Mrs. Clarke will have lunch for you. She has been cooking all day. I know she's excited to have another woman in the house."

"So you know my boss?"

"Of course I know him. Not my business to tell you. You must know he's a big-shot celebrity, but you'll find out more soon enough. Just a pity what happened to him."

"What happened to him?"

"He has a problem with his leg and hand. He's not walking properly anymore. Keeps to himself most of the time."

"How did he get hurt?"

"I'm sure he'll tell you. I'm not supposed to say much. But I'm sure Mrs. Clarke is going to tell you before you hit the pillow tonight." He laughed. "She's not a bad woman, but she does like to talk a lot. If you want to know anything that's happening on the island, you just have to ask her. She would make a good news reporter." He laughed noisily out loud. He had an infectious laugh, which had her smiling until the car pulled into a long driveway lined with tall palm trees. She then breathed in deeply. "Those palms are so...tall."

"That's why they're called royal palms, miss. You'll find them all over the island."

"There is something stately about them."

"They have been here for more than one hundred years, I've been told. The former owners of the house kept records stating that they were planted in 1854."

"Wow! I didn't realize they were so old. Your employer must be proud of this house."

"He is. Only purchased it a few years ago. He did extensive renovation. It looks real nice."

"So you've only been working here since then."

"No, I worked a small period for the former owner. When he died, his wife sold the house and moved back to England. The new owner asked all the staff if we wanted to stay on."

"That's really nice of him. He seems like a pretty nice person."

"He has his moments."

"Can I see him before I go up to my room?"

"Well, he did give me a message to give you. He's given you a few days off to relax and enjoy the island. He's been really busy, but Mrs. Clarke will let you know when he's ready to begin."

This information surprised her. She'd been looking forward to getting down to work. But maybe a day or two to explore the surroundings would help her adjust before she started working.

The door opened and an elderly woman stepped outside. She wore a multicolored dress, which on anyone else would've looked horrid but on her seemed like the perfect outfit.

"It's wonderful to have another woman in the house," she said as she took Aaliyah's hand and shook it with enthusiasm. "I'm Mrs. Clarke and you must be Ms. Carrington. It's a pleasure to meet you."

"You can call me Aaliyah. Your island is really beautiful and I'm delighted to be here."

"Desmond, she's staying in the guest room just down the corridor from the master bedroom," she said, turning to him. "You can take her there." She paused as Desmond headed for the door. "Of course, you can take her luggage at the same time."

Sheepishly, Desmond turned back. "Sorry, Mrs. Clarke."

"I'm sure you're hungry, dear. As soon as you've freshened up, you can come down to lunch. I haven't eaten yet, so we can get to know each other."

"I'd love to freshen up and yes, I'm hungry. I'm not too thrilled about airline meals, so I ate a good dinner last night. Since I left New York early this morning, I've only had a fruit salad, which held me over during the flight."

"Well, as soon as you've freshened up, just come down the stairs, turn right and you'll come to the kitchen along that corridor."

"I will," Aaliyah replied, stepping into the house while Desmond held the door.

What she saw did not come close to what she'd expected. The outside of the house was beautiful, but the inside was spectacular. Like the island, there was a mixture of the old and the new. The interior designer had added blatantly modern pieces to the obvious colonial trappings of the house.

What she liked most of all were the miniature posters of early African-American movies. Several years ago, she'd seen the Margaret Herrick Library/Edward

Mapp Collection at the Academy of Motion Picture Arts and Sciences. She'd had the pleasure of seeing the originals of some of the posters on the wall.

So her employer was a movie buff. She glanced around to see if she could get a glimpse of anything else of significance, but unless she told Desmond to slow down, that would be impossible. However, she followed him, aware that she'd have time in the next few days to explore the house.

Upstairs, she followed Desmond into her room, but had to refrain from not jumping immediately into the grand four-poster bed.

When he wished her goodbye, she took her shoes off and quickly emptied the contents of her suitcases onto the bed. She then placed her clothes into the closet and dresser.

She headed to the bathroom where she quickly freshened up, promising herself a long, leisurely bath as soon as lunch was over. If she'd not been so hungry and knew that Mrs. Clarke was waiting on her she would have taken a nap, but the sudden growl from her stomach reminded her that she needed to eat.

Downstairs, she followed Mrs. Clarke's instructions, but didn't really need to. She just had to follow the heavenly aroma coming from down the passage-way.

When she stepped into the kitchen, Mrs. Clarke had already set the table. Several dishes of nasal-titillating fare were waiting for her to dig in.

"Good, you're here. Just sit where you want and I'll

join you in a sec. Just putting the finishing touches on the salad."

Aaliyah sat, restraining herself from taking a spoon and starting on the soup, which seemed to beckon her to eat.

However, in a short while, Mrs. Clarke placed two salad bowls on the table and sat.

"I'm sorry to keep you waiting. I know you must be hungry."

"I'll manage, though the smell of the soup almost tempted me to start without you."

"I would not have minded if you'd started without me, but I thought eating together would be a good way to get to know you. Let me say a short prayer, and then we can eat." With that, she rattled off a familiar grace.

From the first mouthwatering spoonful of butternut-squash soup to the cheesecake topped with rum-soaked guavas that had been prepared for dessert, Aaliyah could see why her employer had hired Mrs. Clarke. The woman's cooking was a joyous culinary experience and already Aaliyah was anticipating dinner.

"Mrs. Clarke," she said, "how did you learn to cook like this? You could work in the best restaurants of the world. I have never tasted food so good."

"You're such a sweetheart. I haven't had a compliment like that in ages. When the former owner lived here, they entertained often and would have family and friends from England come to spend time on the island. They loved my food."

"I totally agree with them," Aaliyah commented, taking her final bite of the moist, tangy cheesecake.

"Since the new owner bought the house, the parties and dinners have stopped, but he loves a good meal. Though he's not one for compliments, he pays me well and the look on his face when he has finished a meal says it all. I like things as they are now. I'm getting old in age and don't have the energy to cater for such events anymore."

"I'm glad you're still enjoying what you do. Which school did you attend?"

"Didn't have to go to no fancy culinary school to learn how to cook. My mamma traveled all over the world and taught me everything she knew. She seems to have the knack for cooking, too. Of course, I get some ideas from the Food Network, since there isn't anything else worth watching besides *Scandal.* I love me some Olivia Pope. Of course, Fitz is so hot, he could literally cook my food." She cackled out loud, her generous breasts heaving up and down.

"Then it's a date. We can watch the last episode of the season together. I was hoping I wouldn't have to miss it."

"Everyone around here knows that Thursday night is *Scandal* night. I don't have to put up a Do Not Disturb sign anymore. Even the boss knows that Thursday is my off night, so dinner must be eaten early."

"My sister and her best friend are just as obsessed. They come to my house every Thursday."

"You don't see too many shows with strong black

women these days. I remember watching *Julie* with Dianne Carroll years ago. Now that was some show."

"I remember my mom watching it, too. She used to watch a lot of old shows with us."

"She's passed away?" Mrs. Clarke asked softly.

"Yes, my dad and mom died in an accident when I was fourteen. I lived in foster care until I turned eighteen."

"You were an only child?"

"No, I have three sisters. Fortunately, they were all adopted. I recently reconciled with my sister Eboni. But we still haven't found the others."

"Oh, sweetheart, that's so sad. To be separated from them must be awful. Are you looking for the others?"

"Yes, but it's difficult since they were adopted. I have no idea where they are. I don't even know if their names were changed."

"I am sure you'll find them." She raised her hand to the air.

"I just hope they were in good homes."

"I'm sure they were," Mrs. Clarke reassured her. "I noticed that you're married. Couldn't help but see the wedding ring."

"I'm sad news all around, I'm afraid. My husband died three years ago. I'm a widow."

"Oh, dear. Your life has not been easy. I'm sure things are going to look up for you soon. The island is the perfect place to start over. By the time you leave here you'll be ready to live again. Though you must miss your husband."

"Yes, I still miss him. I met him in my last foster home and we were friends since the first day I arrived. He protected me and it just seemed the right thing to do—get married."

"Well, dear. You have a few months to breathe in some clean fresh air, eat some great food and enjoy the island."

"Don't forget I'm here to work," Aaliyah reminded her.

"I haven't forgotten, but when you're not working with him, you'll be able to do all those things, along with watching *Scandal* with me on Thursday nights."

Aaliyah laughed in response to Mrs. Clarke's own laughter.

"See, you're already laughing. Life is too short to be sad about things we can't control or change." She reached over and squeezed Aaliyah's hand. "However, I know that right now you must be tired. You go take a shower and get some rest. I'll call you down for dinner around seven o'clock."

"Thanks. I am feeling a bit tired. Hopefully, a nice bath and some rest will help."

"Good, you go on ahead. I have to start planning tonight's dinner."

Aaliyah rose from the chair. "Thanks for the wonderful lunch. Do you know if I'll get to meet the boss tonight?"

"I'm not sure, but when he's ready to see you, he will."

With that, Mrs. Clarke rose and headed to the sink.

Who on earth was her patient? Aaliyah wondered. This assignment was getting more mysterious by the minute.

* * *

That evening, Dominic watched as his new therapist walked down the corridor. He'd heard the footsteps coming up the stairs as he'd been about to step
through his bedroom door. He'd been on his way
down to visit his beloved puppy before he went to
sleep, a nightly ritual, which he thoroughly enjoyed.

Some nights he'd take Nugget on a walk above the
cliffs. Other nights, he'd stay with the pup until he
fell asleep on his lap. He could not imagine his life
without the pup and remembered his reluctance when
Desmond had first brought the tiny bundle home, just
a few weeks after he'd arrived on the island. He had
no time for cute furry animals, but when the shivering puppy had looked up at him with wide-eyed innocence and licked his hand, it melted his heart.

He'd taken the pup gently in one hand, and since
then a day had not passed without spending time with
his adoring companion.

He watched as the tall, slender frame disappeared
into the room, before he stepped outside. He'd seen
her from the time she'd arrived at his home. He'd
stood behind the curtains, watching as Mrs. Clarke
had greeted her. She'd been polite and he'd seen a
glimpse of white teeth when she'd smiled at something Mrs. Clarke had said.

But he'd seen her before. When Charles had given
her name, he'd done a search on Facebook and an attractive twenty-eight-year-old had appeared on the
screen.

He'd noticed she'd been married, but her eyes reminded him of Nugget's. There was an innocence about her that made it hard for him to imagine she'd been married. She looked naive and untouched and he wondered why Charles chose to burden him with her.

He enjoyed being surrounded not only by beautiful people, but women he could flirt with. And then he remembered… That was all in the past. Who wanted to flirt with a broken man? He was still attractive, but no woman in her right mind would want to be saddled with a man who walked with a cane and ate with their left hand because they couldn't do much with their right.

He headed down the corridor as fast as he could, exiting through the door at the back of the house silently. He didn't want to wake Mrs. Clarke, who, he knew, spent most of her time watching television, or should he say the television watched her, since she would inevitably fall asleep. Unless, of course, it was *Scandal* on the television.

He wondered if she would be surprised to learn he'd watched every episode, as well. His initial attraction had been to the show's star, Kerry Washington, but he'd started to enjoy the witty, tense dialogue, the diversity of characters and the absolute sinfulness of the show. It was one of his few guilty pleasures and one he had no plans to give up.

Outside, he walked over the rocky pathway, which led to the enclosed area where he kept his dogs. Only Nugget and an older dog, Grimm, were outside. His other dog, Rogue, was presently at the vet, after coming down with a very bad virus.

As always when he opened the gate, Nugget was already waiting, his tail wagging. Grimm, on the other hand, stuck her nose up, opened a single eye and closed it again. She was too sleepy to go anywhere and, of course, Desmond was the one who took care of her. Dominic was not much of a dog lover, until Nugget.

Nugget followed him toward the gardens. He knew the dog loved to walk along the cliff, but tonight he did not feel like walking the distance. His leg had been blatantly uncooperative today, so walking in the gardens at the front of the house seemed to be a better alternative.

Nugget loved to race back and forth across the lawn, so Dominic sat on one of the benches dotted across the grounds and watched him play.

He loved it here. He hadn't thought he would, but returning home was the best decision he'd made since his accident. On nights like this, he would sit in the gardens and listen to the sounds of the night.

The shrill cry of crickets and the strident whistle of night frogs combined to create an unexpected tropical orchestra that never ceased to comfort him.

He watched as Nugget successfully ran races against himself. Then for a while the dog disappeared to take care of nature before racing back over to him.

"Time for bed, boy. Let's go."

He stood, heading in the direction of the kennels, and Nugget followed reluctantly behind.

He opened the kennel door and placed the dog inside. With one final look at disappointment, Nugget entered his kennel.

Dominic stood there for a while before he headed back to the house. He'd take a bath and decide if he'd introduce himself to Aaliyah in the morning.

He wasn't looking forward to the therapy, but Charles had insisted.

He was sure she'd be gone in no time. He didn't want anyone intruding upon his quite uneventful life. He was quite happy with things the way they were.

Aaliyah stood on the balcony, looking up at the perfect crescent moon hanging in the crystal-clear sky. Millions and millions of stars twinkled above, reminding her of a childhood rhyme.

There was a noise below her, and she looked down and noticed a man walking jerkily with a cane.

She wondered if it was the man she had come to the island to work for, but the cane was evidence enough. What was he doing outside at this time of night?

She held her breath, hoping that he would look up. She wanted to see him, see his face.

He didn't. Instead, he continued on his way.

When he was gone, her body relaxed. She didn't understand, but her body had reacted to him strangely.

She turned and walked slowly back inside.

Chapter 3

The east coast of the island stretched for miles in the distance. Aaliyah looked back, ensuring that she could still see the house. She'd left the chill of New York behind and welcomed the sunshine, which warmed her. She raised her hands in the air, feeling as if she should burst into a tropical version of The Sound of Music, despite the lack of mountainous terrain. Unexpectedly, a breeze blew in from the ocean, swirling around her, causing her to shiver with the unexpected chill.

She laughed out loud, feeling like a little child who'd discovered something strange and wonderful.

The barking of a dog startled her. She scanned the surroundings, noticing a man sitting on a large rock about fifty meters away overlooking the sea.

A dog, hidden by the rock, emerged and glanced in her direction.

For a moment, it stopped barking, a curious look on its face.

Its tail began to wag and then it charged in her direction. She didn't particularly like dogs, but the look of delight on its face made her smile.

When the small dog reached her, it stopped, lowered its haunches to the ground and looked up at her with expectation. It was a pug, fawn in color.

She knelt and reached to ruffle behind its ears. With a bark of pure delight, it rolled over to expose his stomach.

She tickled him, watching as his eyes closed and a look of pure pleasure appeared.

"Nugget, come over here!" a voice boomed in their direction.

Nugget stood immediately, glanced at her with a sorrowful look and then raced toward the man.

Aaliyah followed, wondering if she were doing the right thing, but any man with a cute small dog couldn't be half bad.

When she reached the man on the rock, he was not facing her direction. When he did, he did so slowly, his gaze vacant, while his eyes caressed her, moving from her legs and up to her face.

At first he didn't say anything, but tilted his head, staring at her cautiously. An unkempt moustache and beard covered his face, but his eyes intrigued her. Dark chocolate, they were expressionless, as if he'd not smiled for a long time.

He stood, holding on to the rock with one hand. He was tall and trim, his muscles rippling under the gray tank top he wore. His broad shoulders tapered down to a narrow waist.

"Hi, I'm Aaliyah."

He did not respond but continued to stare at her, as if he was probing her soul. Her body shivered under his gaze.

"I'm Dominic," he said eventually. His voice was cool but courteous. He turned to the dog. "This is Nugget."

"Nice to meet you, Dominic," she responded politely. "Nugget and I are already good friends. I didn't mean to intrude."

"No problem," he reassured. "You're not on private property."

"Well, it was nice to meet you," she said, turning to pet the dog.

"Are you visiting the island on holiday?" he asked.

"No, I'm here to work. I'm a therapist. I'm staying over there." She pointed in the direction of the house.

"You're staying at the Mansion."

"The Mansion?"

"Yes, that's what we call it around here."

She didn't particularly like the name. It sounded generic and did nothing to describe the beauty of the house.

"Well, I have to go." She glanced down at her watch. "It's getting dark quickly."

He nodded, scrutinizing her. Heat washed over her.

She felt warm and tingly inside. For a moment heat flashed in his eyes, and then it was gone.

She reached for the dog, giggling when he licked her finger.

"I'll see you around, Nugget."

She nodded, turned and walked away. When she'd covered some distance, she turned around. Nugget was looking in her direction, his tail wagging playfully. His master was standing, his back to her, as he looked out to the sea.

When she arrived back at the house, the housekeeper informed her that dinner was ready.

She rushed up to the bedroom, took a shower and raced back downstairs. The walk along the cliff had left her hungry. She'd acquired a hearty appetite during her two days on the island.

Ten minutes later, when she walked into the dining room, she was surprised to see no one there.

She was about to leave and head for the kitchen when Mrs. Clarke entered.

"Oh, good. I'm glad you came down for dinner. I'm getting accustomed to the company."

"I don't like eating alone, either," she responded. She did enjoy the older lady's company.

"Is the owner coming down for dinner?" Aaliyah asked.

"I knew you would ask, but he rarely comes down for dinner." Mrs. Clarke responded softly, as if she feared that someone would hear. "He doesn't feel comfortable eating around others with his hand as it is."

She didn't say more, only indicated that Aaliyah should sit.

When they were both seated, Mrs. Clarke said the blessing.

"I hope you don't mind eating local?" she said, lifting the covers off the dishes.

"I'm fine with whatever you cook," Aaliyah reassured. "I've enjoyed every meal I've had so far. I am looking forward to sampling the local cuisine. Everything looks scrumptious."

"Then you and I will get along royally. He's not too particular about what he eats, either, as long as it tastes good, so I get to cook whatever I fancy. Which I love. I can cook most anything. Italian, English, Spanish, Mexican, you name it, I have recipes up here," she said, touching the top of her head.

"So when will I be able to start work?" Aaliyah asked. Following Mrs. Clarke's lead, she reached for a bowl of salad and spooned rice and garlic potatoes onto her plate.

"I expect he'll come down tomorrow," Mrs. Clarke finally said. "He's a stubborn man, so you'll just have to wait until he thinks it's time."

"Fair enough," Aaliyah replied. She wouldn't force the issue, but it seemed as if she was playing a waiting game with her reluctant patient. "What can you tell me about his injuries?"

"Didn't Dr. Graham tell you?"

"I know it's his leg and his hand. I was thinking more about how they've affected him. Why is he so reluctant to have therapy?"

"Maybe that's something you should talk to him about. He's a very private man."

"Mrs. Clarke, I want to do everything I can to help him. While there are some things he may share with me, the fact that he's so reluctant means he's not going to share his feelings easily. Anything you can tell me will help. Just what you've observed. I'm not asking you to tell me his secrets."

It didn't take Mrs. Clarke any more prompting. By the time Aaliyah retired to her room, she had a better understanding of her patient. She was excited to meet him and begin his treatment. She'd been given his files and knew she could help him. He just had to be willing to work, and based on what Mrs. Clarke and Dr. Graham had told her, she had her job cut out for her.

She wondered what could have prompted Dr. Graham to think that she could handle this patient. The enthusiasm she'd experienced when she'd decided to take on this job was slowly waning.

His reluctance to start the session was beginning to exasperate her. She would give him one more day and then she planned on doing something about it.

What she was going to do? She wasn't even sure. But she had no intention of waiting too much longer.

There was a knock on the door. Dominic picked his cane up and walked slowly to the door.

"Who is it?" he shouted.

"It's only me," Mrs. Clarke responded. "I need to speak to you, Mr. Wolfe."

He opened the door slowly, suspecting that she was about to reprimand him again.

He stepped back, letting her enter.

"I know what you're here about," he said. He gave an impatient shrug.

"Do not make assumptions, young man." Her eyes sparked. "But yes, I'm here about the young lady who keeps asking where her patient is. She's getting a bit worried and I suspect she's soon going to file a missing person's report."

"I would think she'd been happy to enjoy her first few days doing nothing but enjoying our wonderful sunshine. Most women would," he said, his voice heavy with sarcasm.

"I'm sure most would." She shook her head in dismay. "Unfortunately, she is not most women, she is here to do a job. You're going to have to meet with her and start your sessions. I would think your priority would be to get better."

"I suspect that this may be an attempt to make me believe that I can get better. It's been almost a year since the fire and I'm no closer to being better than I was six months ago."

"And whose fault is that?" she reasoned. "If you persist in being as nonchalant about your injuries and your recovery, what do you expect?"

He glared at her, shocked that she'd had the gall to speak to him that way. But then he saw the glimmer of tears in her eyes, and the sense of despair and frustration.

She was right. He was being stubborn about this

situation, despite his promise to Charles that he would try this time.

"Okay, I'll meet with her tomorrow and then decide where to go from there," he said calmly.

Nodding her approval, she wished him good-night and stepped outside, closing the door behind her.

He walked back to the chair next to his bed and sat. He did find his new therapist intriguing and the fact that she was pleasant to the eye made her that much more appealing.

So tomorrow he'd take the time to introduce himself...again. He could already imagine the look on her face when she discovered they'd already met.

He could have done the right thing then and introduced himself, but he hadn't been ready. Acknowledging her would be to acknowledge the possibilities.

He didn't want possibilities. He wanted a definite. Why should he go to all the trouble to exert himself when the outcome could leave him just as he was? There were no guarantees after all.

Dominic headed for the shower. Tonight he'd go to bed early. It seemed as though he'd have to face the future...and a reality that he wasn't sure he could handle.

Smoke billowed around him. He could not breathe, but he had to climb the stairs. While the fire had not spread yet to this part of the house, the stifling grayness slowed his progress. He'd had the good sense to soak the small towel with the contents of the bottle of water he'd had in the car.

In the distance, he heard the sound of sirens. Good, they'd be here soon. And then he heard another sound, almost like the cry of a wounded animal. It must be the little girl.

He pushed the door open, but it refused to budge. He pushed again and this time it creaked open, the hinges stiff from lack to oil.

When he entered the room, he searched for movement in the thickening smoke but could not find her.

"Where are you?" he shouted.

"I'm in the bathroom," the voice replied, followed by a bout of coughing.

"I'm coming to get you."

"Please hurry. I'm scared."

He walked along the wall, feeling until his hands touched the door. He pushed it open.

The little girl immediately hurled herself at him. He loosened the cloth around his mouth and nose and tied it around hers, telling her to only breathe when she needed to.

He lifted her up and headed in the direction he'd come, but when he stepped into the hallway, the flames greeted him. He could feel the heat beneath him and above. He turned around and headed in the other direction, not sure where it would lead.

And then he heard it—a loud creaking beneath him. Suddenly, he found himself falling into heat and darkness.

Dominic bolted awake. He'd been dreaming again. He cursed the night. When was this going to end?

He'd saved the girl, so why was he being tortured by the memory of that night?

Everyone thought he was a hero. So why couldn't he get a good night's sleep without the heat and pain of the memory?

He rose from the bed, stepping onto the floor, pulling his left leg back when a sharp pain raced along it. He fell back to the bed, sweat pouring from his body, and waited until the pain subsided to the annoying throb he'd grown accustomed to.

When he could finally stand, he shifted to the chair and picked up his iPad and started to read.

It was only in the early hours of the morning, just before the sun rose, that he crawled back into bed and fell asleep.

Chapter 4

Aaliyah looked out to sea. Today the waves tossed angrily. On the horizon, dark clouds swirled. She could tell it was going to rain. The day had passed uneventfully. When she'd asked about her still mysterious patient that morning, Mrs. Clarke had told her he'd be meeting with her sometime during the day. She'd felt like screaming but instead had slowly walked away.

After spending her day reading and watching the afternoon talk shows, she'd found herself heading to the cliff, wondering if she'd see the dog again. She didn't particularly care to see the man.

She turned abruptly back toward the house when the first drop of water touched her.

She started to run, taking her time along the rocky

area. By the time she reached the house, her clothes clung to her.

She stood on the verandah, wondering what to do.

A throat clearing startled her and she turned in the direction of the sound.

The man sat on a chair. Next to him, the dog sat, its tail thumping on the floor.

"What are you doing here?" she demanded. For some strange reason, her heart pounded against her chest, almost in harmony with the rain.

"Seeking shelter from the rain. I decided it would be smarter to get back before the rain came."

His sarcasm stung, but he was right. She'd known that the rain would come. She'd allowed herself to be controlled by her desire to see him again.

Who on earth was he? And then it dawned on her. The man sitting down was her boss, her patient. If she'd been observant, she would have noticed the cane lying on the floor.

"You're my patient?" she exclaimed.

He paused, his eyes twinkling with laughter. "I confess. I am your...boss."

A word she didn't often use sprung to her head, but she prided herself with self-control and the word remained a thought.

"I was beginning to wonder if you'd ever appear," she said. Her disapproval was subtle, but her message was clear.

"Oh, I planned on appearing eventually. Now is a bit premature, but what's done is done." He shrugged in mock resignation. "I wanted you to give you a few days to enjoy the island before you started work. And of course, I needed to adjust to a new intrusion in my life. Charles just doesn't seem to realize I'm fine."

"It would have been polite to meet me the day I arrived and explain that," she said.

"Didn't Mrs. Clarke pass on the information?" he asked.

She almost screamed in exasperation. He was such a pain in the ass already. But he was her boss. Respect was important.

"Yes, I did get the message."

"So what's the problem?"

"I'm here to work, so I expect to do exactly that."

She moved closer to him, feeling that moment of familiarity again. His face was so familiar.

And then it came.

He was Dominic Wolfe! *People* magazine had named him one of the sexiest men alive.

"I can see you recognize me now."

"I'm sorry. I didn't realize. Dr. Graham didn't tell me."

"Does it make a difference?" he challenged.

She hesitated briefly. "No, it doesn't. I'm just here to do a job that you don't seem to want me to do. But you could have told me yesterday that you were my boss."

"Oh, I was just having some fun with you. You would have found out in time."

Again she paused then said, "I don't want to be rude, *boss*," she said sarcastically, "but I really want to find out when I start your therapy."

He smiled widely, and then stood. He reached for the cane on the floor.

"I'll get back to you on that." He then turned and trudged away, the dog following behind him.

He was in pain. She could tell, but she suspected it was pure pride.

She shivered, glancing down and realizing that she was still wearing the wet clothing, which emphasized her firm breasts and the nipples straining against the fabric.

She walked in the direction he'd disappeared to, glancing toward the pathway. He and the dog were walking away from the house.

The rain had abated, and she watched as he walked away. She'd noticed that despite his smile and teasing, his eyes were dull and lifeless, almost as if he'd given up on ever enjoying life again.

She knew she had her work cut out for her, but the healer inside was already reaching out to him.

His legs hurt. His legs always hurt, but walking along the cliff's face for a short period allowed him to be free from his troubled thoughts.

He was angry. Still angry about what had happened to him. He'd tried to forget, but the memories came while he lay in bed at night, tossing and turning, unable to sleep.

He didn't regret how the accident had come about. He'd saved the little girl's life, but the pain in his side and his limp were a constant reminder of the changes he'd had to endure when it came to the life he used to have. A life he wanted back.

When he reached the cliff's edge, he hobbled to the large rock where he usually sat. The walk from the house was good exercise for his leg and while it worried him, it was his useless hand that worried him more. Externally the hand had healed, though a slight scar served as a reminder of the series of surgeries. He did have some mobility, but he could not lift anything too heavy, nor could he bend his fingers without pain.

The rain had finally stopped falling. When he'd left the veranda, it had still been drizzling, but from the clouds and wind, he'd known that it would soon stop. Now the ocean breeze and the dampness of his shirt caused him to shiver.

One of the things he liked about living on the island was what he saw before him. There was nothing more beautiful than looking out to sea. He'd soon have to get back to the house, since darkness approached swiftly. But for a few minutes each day, he looked across the ocean, reminding himself that he'd come a long way from the poor little boy who'd raced along this same cliff as a little child. Ironically, in those days, he'd stared at the big house in the distance he dreamed of owning one day.

When the owners of the house had put it up for sale a few years ago, he'd heard about it and immediately sent his lawyer to buy it.

Though he'd owned it for several years, he'd never used it. Instead, he offered it to friends who wanted to come to the island for holiday. The island reminded him too much of the boy he'd been, the boy who'd fallen asleep with the pain in his stomach gnawing at his insides.

When he'd come out of hospital just over six months ago, Charles had agreed he should come back here. Reluctantly, he had.

Now he couldn't think of being anywhere else. The island he'd known had in a short space of time worked its magic. As a child he'd seen the island through the eyes of a young, troubled boy.

When his mother had passed away and he'd moved to the United States, things had changed.

Going to the Armani section of Macy's had been the proverbial being in the right place at the right time. He'd taken to going into stores where designer clothes were sold. One day, he'd taken the money he'd saved all summer to buy a few outfits.

His well-toned body had attracted the attention of a woman in the store. She'd given him a business card and invited him to a meeting in her office. The next day, he'd arrived at The Crane Agency, wearing one of the new outfits he'd purchased the previous day.

That day, Chandra Crane, owner of one of the largest, most influential modeling agencies in New York, had signed him to an exclusive contract. The rest was history.

At his feet, Nugget barked. He reached down to trace his right hand through Nugget's silky coat. The dog's eyes were on him, his tongue hanging out.

When he straightened up, he grasped his cane,

heading back to the house. He wanted to go to his workshop. He needed to create. Nugget followed.

When he stepped inside the room, a familiar feeling of dread and anxiety slammed him in the stomach, but as he always did, he fought the swelling, stifling emotion. He walked over to the workbench and settled himself on the stool. A lump of clay sat on the sculpturing stand, as it had for the past two weeks. He reached out, placing his right hand on the clay, feeling its warmth.

He longed to work the clay. Already he could see the image in his head transforming under his hand. He reached out his other hand, watching as it moved slowly toward the clay, collapsing onto the misshaped lump. He willed his fingers to move, but nothing happened, only the excruciating pain racing along his arms and then to the tips of his fingers. Tears of frustration formed in his eyes as he closed and opened them again.

His good hand swiped across the table. Clay and tools flew across the room.

A word his mom would have washed his mouth with soap for slipped from his lips. He hated cursing. Had never done it. His mother's teachings had stuck with him until recently.

A wave of shame washed over him, but he forced it away. This is different. He was different. Fate had taken hold of his life. He felt battered and helpless.

Slowly his thoughts drifted to his therapist. Already she frustrated him with her prim and proper demeanor. She was pretty, in a conventional kind of way, if you were willing to look beyond the cool exterior.

She was definitely not his type. In his celebrity days, he'd been seen with some of the most beautiful starlets. He counted in his head. He couldn't remember the last time he'd made love. For a while after his accident, a few of his "friends" had visited him in the hospital, but when the days had stretched into weeks and then months, the visits had trickled to a complete stop. The only person who'd continued his visits had been Dr. Graham, his doctor and friend.

He'd met Charles Graham in high school. Ironically, in class they had battled constantly for academic superiority, and while he'd often won, his career choice had taken him in a totally different direction. Despite that, they'd become friends. When he'd arrived at the hospital after the accident, he'd been surprised to see Charles there. Charles had immediately taken over his case and over the past year they had become much closer friends. Charles had been the one to give him his first glimmer of hope. In the hands of a lesser surgeon, the hope of walking and using his hand again might have been just that: a hope.

There was a knock at the door. Reluctantly, he responded.

He rose slowly, not wanting the individual to see the mess he'd made. He'd clean it up later.

He moved laboriously to the door, stopping to breathe in deeply.

He pushed the door open. It was Mrs. Clarke.

"What's wrong?" he said, observing the concerned look on her face.

"It's after dinnertime and you haven't come down."

"Sorry, I'll eat in my room tonight."

"You plan on ignoring the young lady for the rest of the week? Didn't you tell me last night you were going to meet with her today?"

"I don't particularly want her here," he snapped. "It's only because Dr. Graham insisted."

"But don't you want to be better?"

"I tried," he stated firmly.

"No, you've given up," she replied. "You have given up."

"Can we not talk about this anymore?" He set his chin in a stubborn line.

"Promise me you will at least give her a chance. Maybe her touch is what you need," she said, a broad smile on her face.

He did not smile in return.

She sighed in frustration.

"You do realize she's pretty. Maybe having a beautiful woman around will have a positive effect on you."

"Beautiful?" He laughed. "Have you seen the women I've dated?"

"I know the women you kept company with. Tell me, where are they now? Beauty is more than external."

"Please," he pleaded, "I'm really not up to this. Can you just send my dinner up?"

"Okay. I'm sorry." Her shoulders sagged in defeat.

"Don't want to put you under any more pressure. But I worry about you."

"I'll be fine."

"Well, you go ahead and do what you're doing. I'll send your dinner up. Where are you going to be?"

"In my room."

"Okay, but if you don't come down tomorrow morning to meet with that nice young lady, I'm coming for you myself."

"I promise," he said reluctantly.

"Good," she responded. "I'll hold you to that promise."

With that, she turned and walked away.

He watched her leave. He was glad she chose to remain on staff. She was like a mother hen, hovering around him, but he knew that she cared. Not many people in his life truly cared about him.

At least he knew one little girl out there who cared for him. And if he had to do it over, he'd save her again, without hesitation.

But he did not fail, in the middle of the night, to question the irony of his situation. It had been only a few months after *People* had named him the sexiest man alive that he'd lost it all. He wasn't sexy anymore… That was for sure.

One of the things he'd discovered about himself was the fact that he'd become vain and arrogant. He thought about his first few weeks in hospital and the way he'd treated the staff. In time he'd become just any other patient. His "friends" had disappeared; the reporters and the fans had all vanished, leaving him totally alone.

He shook his head, trying to purge the memories. He was doing what he could, living each day as it came. There were no jobs, no special one…just him.

He glanced down at the lump of clay and saw an image forming in his mind. He wanted to lay his hands on the clay and watch it come alive.

But he knew, even without much thought, that his dream was impossible.

Maybe he should start therapy tomorrow morning.

He sighed. He didn't want to go. He was sure that this therapist would only tell him what he didn't want to hear: that the life he'd known was no longer.

He reached down, gripped the cane and breathed in deeply, waiting for the familiar surge of pain as he started to walk.

Inside he screamed his hurt. At least the fact that there was pain meant that he was still alive.

Chapter 5

Aaliyah stood on the balcony. In the distance she could see the white-and-red stripes of a lighthouse peeping through the single mahogany tree just beyond her bedroom. She was surprised things were so peaceful here on the island, but Mrs. Clarke had informed her that the house was on the eastern part of the island. To the west lay the city of Bridgetown, the capital and center of commerce.

She hoped to visit the city sometime, but for now she was content with the tranquility of the more rural part of the island.

Below her, a dog barked. She glanced down. She was glad to know she was not the only one awake. Nugget began to bark loudly and then reappeared... with *him*.

Her heart stopped.

Even from where she stood, there was no denying that he was handsome. Gone was his unkempt beard. He looked raw, sexy and all male.

She gasped.

His head slowly tilted upward.

Their eyes locked. Unexpected heat coursed through her, leaving her hot and flustered. He nodded, and then placed his focus on the lively puppy racing between his legs. His deep laughter floated up to her.

She stepped back, uncomfortable with the feelings assaulting her. She'd only met the man a few days ago and already she was having naughty, erotic thoughts about him. She hadn't made love since her husband had passed away, and that was one of the things she'd missed most. Lovemaking between her and her husband had been perfect. They'd become lovers in their late teens when they'd left the foster home and decided to move in together.

They'd both been smart, and had obtained scholarships and decided to go to Columbia. She thought back to the night they'd made love for the first time. Andrew had been wild, bold and daring, but he'd also been warm and sensitive. She'd entered the apartment and found the lights all off, the only light coming from candles on the floor. She'd followed the flickering lights into the bedroom and found him on the bed, butt naked and fast asleep, a single rose clutched in his grasp.

She'd not had a hint of what he had been planning when she'd called him half an hour before to let him know she was on her way home. She'd gone in, taken a shower, and when she was done, shook him awake. They'd spent the rest of the night making love. In the early hours of the morning, he'd proposed and she'd happily accepted.

She walked over to the bed and sat as tears formed in her eyes and trickled down her cheeks. She missed him so much. At times the pain of missing him was so intense she couldn't sleep. The memory of his scent would be so strong that she wondered if he was nearby.

But that was starting to change; his scent was beginning to fade into a distant memory.

She stood and glanced at the clock and realized that it was already seven. She wanted to eat breakfast before she headed to the gym for her first session with Dominic.

She slipped off the robe she was wearing and changed into a T-shirt and a pair of jeans.

When she reached the dining room several minutes later, she found herself alone, as usual.

Mrs. Clarke entered the room shortly after.

"Mr. Wolfe has already eaten. He's gone upstairs to dress for the session."

"Thanks for letting me know. I'm looking forward to working with him."

"I'm hoping it works out this time. He's had a bad time with the others. None of them seemed to be able to reach him. But I have my bets on you."

"I'm glad you have confidence in me. I hope I can live up to your expectations."

"Honey, I am sure you are going to. Well, you sit and have some breakfast. You have a hard session in front of you." With that, she giggled sweetly and left the room.

Aaliyah grimaced. She had no doubt that Mrs. Clarke's prediction would come true. In fact, since her career change, none of her patients had been receptive to the schedule she'd imposed on them. In fact, most of them were still upset with the world and what it had done to them. But eventually she would break through their barriers and they would work hard at healing and look forward to their long journey.

She walked over to the buffet table, picked up a plate and filled it with scrambled eggs and bacon, and placed two slices of bread in the toaster. She added sliced mango, apples and pineapple to a smaller plate and sat to nibble on the fruit while waiting for the toast to be done. She ate slowly, especially savoring the mangoes, a favorite fruit of hers.

When she was done with the meal, she raced upstairs to brush her teeth and then headed in the direction of the gym that Mrs. Clarke had pointed out earlier.

When she reached the room, she knocked.

He was already there.

And looked incredibly gorgeous.

He was sitting on one of the machines, his legs stretched out in front of him. He wore no shirt, and her eyes immediately lowered to his abs—a complete six-pack. While his body was not as toned as it could be, with a little effort he'd be back to his trim, fit celebrity self. And it was not that he was lacking anything—he redefined sexy.

She could not keep her eyes off of the hair that started at his navel and trickled below the band of his shorts.

"I'm all ready to begin," he said. She could hear the hint of sarcasm in his voice.

"So am I," she replied cheerfully. She walked over to where he sat.

"I'm going to establish a routine which we'll use for each of our sessions. We'll start off with some stretches, then some work on the machines and finally we'll focus on the muscles of your weaker leg and hand."

"Sounds fine to me. I'm so looking forward to this." She heard the same sarcasm in his voice.

"Along with the exercises, we're going to have to do some work on your attitude. A pleasant disposition is the key to positive progress." She grimaced. She was beginning to sound like a schoolmarm.

"A lady that knows how to be witty. I like that in a woman."

She tried to ignore him but the look on his face made her want to laugh. Instead, she held her composure.

For the next half an hour she took him through the stretches and some exercises to strengthen his leg. He did them with the enthusiasm of a bored schoolboy, and with each exercise came complaints.

When he was done, she tossed him a towel from

one of the benches in the gym and told him to get un-
dressed and wrap himself in the towel.

What he did next left her flabbergasted, flustered…
and hot.

Standing in front of her, he placed a hand on the
waistband of his shorts and pulled them down in one
smooth, fluid movement.

She gasped.

He looked up.

She turned around, but not before she caught a
glimpse of his generous manhood.

"You can turn around now," he said. She could
hear the amusement in his voice.

She turned slowly. Her face still flushed with her
embarrassment.

"You could have warned me you were planning to
do a striptease," she chided.

"Sorry, I thought you with you being medical per-
sonal, that shouldn't surprise you."

She breathed deeply, wanting to focus on the job
ahead. "Please lie on the bed over there," she said,
ignoring his comment.

He complied without hesitation, though getting on
the bed did require her assistance.

Her first touch was firm. She kneaded his muscles
gently, rubbing in a warm liquid.

Her hands were not as soft as he'd expected, but
firm and strong. He felt the warm moistness of the
liquid she'd poured on him. She then began to massage his muscles with a more firm approach.

And then things started to change for him. The hands started to feel different.

The tightened muscles, the throbbing pain that had become part of his existence slowly dissipated. All he could think of was the sensation flowing through him from her touch. He couldn't remember the last time he'd had a woman's hands on his body, but even then, he couldn't remember it feeling this good. He closed his eyes and felt himself drifting.

When he awoke, he was alone. Damn, he'd fallen asleep, but he still felt tired from the lack of sleep. He knew it would take him a while to adjust to this new routine. He rarely slept in the darkness of the night, but found that with the light the memories faded and he was able to sleep without the nightmare that haunted him.

One of the reasons he'd given her the first few days off. He'd been trying to force himself to sleep so he could be awake early in the morning.

He rose from the bed, realizing the towel had fallen to the floor. He chuckled, noting that he had already given her a special showing of his equipment.

What the hell had possessed him to do that? She'd probably call the police and accuse him of sexual harassment.

He lowered his feet to the ground, his right foot first to take the weight of the left.

While he felt some pain, it was not the same excruciating pain that usually followed his first step.

Instead, he experienced a different type of numbness that was more bearable.

Even his body felt better. Maybe Charles was right. She seemed to know what she was doing and, in fact, this was the best he'd felt since returning home.

Her touch was magical. In more ways than one. As she'd kneaded his sore muscles, he'd found his body responding and had tried to control it by thinking of something else. Fortunately it had worked.

He glanced at the clock on the wall. It was time for lunch.

Should he eat lunch with Aaliyah or in his room?

It was probably better if he went back to his room. He was sure she wouldn't be too happy to face him after their session.

Several minutes later, Mrs. Clarke informed him that Aaliyah was not feeling well and would remain in her room for the rest of the day.

What had he done?

Chapter 6

The next morning before sunrise, Dominic walked along the cliff's face. As memories of running along these cliffs during his childhood tried to surface, he pushed them into the back of his mind, where he kept them buried. There were few memories from that period of life that he found pleasant.

It was not that he didn't love his mother, but he'd hated being poor. He remembered the nights he went to bed hungry and the hours it had taken for him to fall asleep.

He did not want to go back there. As he looked out to sea, he felt the same emotions now. This had been a place of refuge for him. It was here where he'd forgotten about his life and fantasized about a better life.

In the distance, he could see the rooftops of the

houses of the village where he had grown up. Since he'd arrived on the island, he'd refused to go back there. He wondered if anyone there would remember him. He wondered if his childhood best friend, Adrian Johnson, still lived there. He had left the island at fourteen to live with a father he hadn't even known. He'd cried when his mother had passed away, but there had been a kind of relief in those tears. Living in New York had forever changed his life...for the better.

His father was gone now, too, but even before his father's death, he'd had big plans and ideas. His father had been a dreamer, but he'd taken his own dreams and made them come true.

He shook his head, not wanting to go back to that time just a few years ago when life had been perfect. He had been perfect. He'd been the envy of most models. He'd strutted on the runway with confidence, and the fashion world had embraced him with a reverence he didn't quite understand.

He heard a bark in the distance. Nugget had found a crab. The pup loved crabs and could spend hours sitting by a hole waiting for the creatures to emerge. He called the dog, and Nugget immediately raced in his direction, coming to an ungainly stop.

"Come, boy. Let's head back to the house. I have a session with the beautiful Ms. Carrington this morning and I want to be on my best behavior...which means I have to be early for the session."

Nugget looked up, his head cocked to the side, an expression of distinct comprehension on his face.

"Everything she does annoys the pants off me." Not that he didn't find her appealing. In fact, he found her quite attractive. And she smelled good. He wasn't particularly fond of the strong flowery scent most women seemed to prefer. Instead, her subtle scent reminded him of the ocean breeze that even now wafted across the cliff's face.

One minute he was thinking about her, the next he was lying flat on his stomach. Of course, Nugget thought they were playing a game and jumped on his back, barking at the top of his puppy voice.

Pain coursed through his body while the muscles in his leg started to spasm. He lay on the ground unable to move. Slowly, very slowly, the pain subsided. He raised his head, looking around to see if anyone had seen him fall.

He searched around for his cane, finding it with little effort. He used it to rise to his feet, scowling when he jolted it and the pain stung.

He stood, his legs still feeling shaky from the fall.

And then it dawned on him. He had the opportunity to be better, work on being better, and he was being pigheaded. The only person he was hurting with his attitude was himself.

He walked slowly, his thoughts troubled by his revelation. Maybe he needed to take a look at himself. If he'd been the one to observe his behavior he would have been appalled.

When he reached the pathway leading up the back of the house, he slowed down. He hoped no one could tell he'd fallen. Hopefully, he could slip inside without telling the others.

He'd planned on coming down for breakfast, but his legs hurt and a splitting headache was coming on. Nugget whimpered and he looked down. The pup was hungry.

He had no choice but to go to the kitchen. He'd just have to deal with Mrs. Clarke. Hopefully she was the only one there.

When he entered the kitchen a few minutes later, he frowned. It was the drill sergeant. She was drinking a cup of tea and watching the television he'd placed in the kitchen for Mrs. Clarke. "Can't miss my soaps," she'd told him.

He'd placed a large widescreen model that she guarded as if it were some kind of precious gem. No one dared to mess with Mrs. Clarke's television when the soaps or her special morning shows were on.

Before she could speak, Nugget rushed over to where she sat and barked softly as if he didn't want to disturb her.

She glanced up, her gaze immediately coming to rest on him.

"Good morning," she said, stoically. Damn, did she ever smile? Aaliyah was all business at all times and he wondered what she'd do if he were to kiss her. Immediately, he pushed the thought from his mind. He wasn't even sure where it'd come from.

She stood with the cup in her hand, and headed to the sink.

"What's wrong?" she asked, her voice filled with concern. She walked closer to him and stopped.

Her hand reached for his face and she brushed something away.

"You're covered in grass and dust."

He almost cowered but straightened his back.

"It's nothing," he replied. "I'm fine."

"I'm sure you are," she said, her voice tinted with amusement.

He looked at her, standing before him. There was a twinkle in her eyes.

"I'm glad I can be of some amusement to someone."

"I'm not amused. Wonder why you would be so worried about a little fall."

"Fall? I didn't…" He stopped. It didn't make any sense lying. He'd fallen. Period. That was all.

"I have to feed Nugget." He turned to the dog, ignoring her.

"I'm going back to my room. The session is at nine, remember?"

He was about to tell her he wasn't coming but stopped himself. He'd go and show her he wasn't a shirker.

"I'll see you," he stated firmly.

She smiled briefly and left, but not before he saw the hint of smile on her lips.

He growled. She had the uncanny ability to get under his skin.

He walked toward the stairway, still wondering why he'd refused to move to a bedroom downstairs.

Of course, he'd wanted to prove he could be independent. Now each time he labored upstairs, the pain in his leg reminded him how stubborn he'd been.

What seemed like hours later, he entered his room, stripped his clothes off and dressed in his outfit for the session.

He groaned. He was not looking forward to it.

While he knew the importance of the session, he didn't feel comfortable with Aaliyah yet. He felt something stirring between them. Each time she placed her hands on him, it took all of his control not to get rock hard. His response to her still baffled him. It had crept up on him.

It was her touch. There was something exciting and titillating about her hands on him. And she was never anything other than professional.

He was the one with the overactive imagination, the one with the one-track mind. He needed sex. He had not had sex since the accident.

He glanced up at the clock. Time for his session. He sighed. Already his body was reacting in anticipation.

Aaliyah had reached the stage where the word *frustration* didn't come close to explain how she was feeling. She'd balked on several occasions at calling Dr. Graham. While she understood what Dominic was going through, she really thought he was behaving like a spoiled brat.

He was twenty minutes late, which had become his daily routine. She was sure he did it deliberately.

Just to get on her nerves. Just to prove he was the still the boss.

The door creaked and she turned in the direction of the noise. Dominic walked in.

"Sorry to be late," he said.

"I'm sure you are," she retorted.

"I mean it. I'm sorry."

She huffed.

"Now, what does that mean?"

"You've never been early for any of our sessions thus far, so there really isn't any need for you to be sorry. I work for you."

He stared at her and nodded his head slowly. "That's true," he agreed. "So what are the plans for today?"

"We'll go through our regular routine."

He groaned.

"I do have some additional sets to add."

He groaned again. "I know Charles sent you here to torture me."

"Maybe he did. But I think he did because he knows I am good at what I do."

"You like your work?"

"I do. However, we really can't do your exercises if you keep talking. You need to get on the bench."

He signed. She was persistent. Something he liked about her. The other two nurses had given up on him. Aaliyah wasn't too happy about having free days. She'd made it clear that the only days they would be resting were Saturdays and Sundays.

He'd agreed reluctantly. There had been one day

when his sessions had not been too hectic. However, that didn't mean that his body hadn't ached when he went to bed at night.

He looked at her and she returned the stare. He could see her irritation and moved quickly to start the first routine. It was going to be a long morning.

The lunch bell chimed. She didn't think she would ever get accustomed to the bell ringing for meals. It reminded her of high school. She put the folders she was reading aside and walked downstairs to the dining room.

While breakfast could be eaten in the kitchen, Mrs. Clarke insisted they ate lunch and dinner in the dining room.

She didn't particularly mind, since the room opened onto a large patio, which provided a picturesque view of the ocean in the distance. When she stepped into the room she was more than a bit surprised to see Dominic there.

He'd changed out of his gym clothes and wore a white T-shirt and a pair of khaki shorts. She'd seen pictures of him on television and he looked more like that person now.

He'd shaved and shaped up his hairline. He was standing on the patio, his gaze focused on the ocean.

Next to him, Nugget sat, his tail playfully thumping the floor. At her footsteps he stopped, looked up and immediately raced to her, the speed of his tail increasing with each step.

Dominic turned.

Their eyes met, his gaze lingered and she looked away. Her eyes fell to look at the puppy sitting at her feet. She reached down, tickled his ear and watched as he shivered with excitement.

"He likes you." Dominic's voice startled her. She'd not seen him walk over to her but she could now smell the woodsy fragrance of his cologne.

"Mrs. Clarke told me I could start lunch as soon as you arrived."

"You didn't have to wait."

"That would have been rude. You're a guest in my home."

"Well, thanks for waiting. I don't much like eating by myself."

"I have been pretty antisocial, haven't I?" he stated. "I promise I will be a lot more accommodating in future."

"It's fine. I'm really not a guest. I'm working for you, remember? I don't expect to be treated like a guest."

"Then that's how we differ. Anyone who's here at my request is a guest. And since I'm the boss," he chuckled, "I get to determine what I want you to be."

"I can't argue with that," she agreed reluctantly.

"So you're ready to eat? I am starving after the torture you put me through."

"I am hungry. The island air seems to have affected my appetite."

"That's a good thing, isn't it?"

"I'm not sure. I may just have to start using the gym while I'm here."

"Feel free to use it whenever you want. You only work for me in the mornings. Your evenings are yours to do whatever you want."

"I was thinking about that. I'd like us to do a bit of walking during the afternoon a few times a week. I'm sure it will help to make your leg stronger."

"Well, you are the professional. Charles told me I have to do everything you say. It doesn't seem like I have much of a choice."

"But you do. This is all about choices. It shouldn't be about what Charles says. You're the one with the medical problem, not Charles."

"That's true. Then I'll rephrase what I said. I'd be delighted for us to take a walk some afternoons. As long as I can bring Nugget along."

"Of course," she replied. "I wouldn't have it any other way."

"Good, but now we really have to eat. My stomach is growling."

He led her to the table and waited for her to sit before he did.

His gesture surprised her, but she realized she was being unfair. She was casting assumptions on his character and she didn't really know him yet.

Aaliyah could not sleep. Strange, since she'd slept so well from the time she'd arrived on the island. She glanced at the clock. Just after midnight. She needed to get a good night's sleep since she had to be up early in the morning.

The sessions with Dominic had been going well,

though she sensed a bit of reluctance and resistance each time. She'd had three sessions with him already and each day, she felt exhausted at his lack of interest, especially when the massage portion began. Since that first day, he'd not allowed her to complete the session. She wondered if he was in more pain than he admitted.

She sighed, turning restlessly on the bed. She pulled the sheet around her. The central air was at a perfect temperature. But it wasn't hot; she just felt miserable.

She'd been feeling like that a lot lately around Dominic. He left her feeling hot and bothered after each one of their sessions. The image of him naked still flashed in her mind's eye and she almost wished he would drop his clothes again.

She was attracted to him. There was no doubt about it. If she'd known this would happen, she would have returned to New York after their initial session on the next available flight. Maybe that was the only choice she had now.

She sighed. She didn't want to think of this now. She'd go downstairs and get something to drink. Maybe a glass of milk would make her feel better.

She rose from the bed, reaching for her robe on the chair.

She walked along the hallway and when she passed Dominic's room, she heard a noise. It sounded like an animal's cry.

She paused, listening in the silence, and then she heard it again.

A whimper. Maybe it was Nugget, but she'd thought Nugget slept outdoors in the kennels.

The cry increased. She knocked on the door.

When she stepped inside, the flickering light of a single candle welcomed her. In the center, a big-canopied bed appeared to be lost in the spacious room.

Within the folds of the bed, Dominic lay naked, the sheet barely covering his lower body. As she looked down at him, he groaned again and whimpered something.

Then his body crashed and tossed.

She reached out to touch him, shaking him. He jumped awake suddenly, whipping his hands around and striking her on the shoulder.

She winced in pain.

His eyes searched frantically around the room and landed on her.

"What the hell are you doing in here?" he growled.

"I'm sorry. I heard a noise. You were having a nightmare."

"And you had to intrude on my privacy?"

"I'll leave. I thought something was wrong. I apologize."

She turned to walk away.

"I'm sorry."

She turned around, a skeptical smile on her face. "I'm sure you're not usually like this. I look forward to seeing the other you."

He laughed. "I deserved that."

"Yes, you do. I know you don't want me here. But

I'm here and I'm going to make sure I do everything in my power to make sure you get better, whether you believe you will or not."

With that, she turned and walked away.

She headed to the kitchen. She probably needed something stronger that milk to get her to sleep. Hopefully she'd find something a lot more calming. She needed to unwind. She'd been feeling tense for the past few days.

And Dominic Wolfe had a lot to do with her feelings. She could not deny her attraction to him.

Each day she found it more and more difficult to work with him, though only a few days had passed since they'd started.

She walked along the corridor, her footsteps barely heard in the silence.

When she entered the kitchen, she looked around, noticing the cupboard. She headed for the refrigerator, immediately finding the half bottle of wine they'd had at dinner.

She searched for a glass, filled it and sat at the marble-covered island.

She placed the glass to her lips, sipping slowly. Immediately, her body warmed. There was nothing a glass of wine couldn't cure.

Her thoughts strayed to her boss.

Her visit to his room had affected her more than she'd expected. She knew that she would be more tolerant of him. She could still hear his cries of anguish in her head.

He was definitely haunted by something. She wondered if it was the accident. She'd heard about it.

She put the glass down and headed back to her room. When she got there she reached for her iPad, turned it on and opened Google.

She typed in his name and was not surprised when a series of articles popped up. She narrowed the search, inputting *fire*. She clicked on the first link and it took her to a CNN article. His face looked back at her.

She lay on the bed, taking the iPad with her. For the next thirty minutes, she read all she could about him. By the time she closed her eyes, she was satisfied with what she had learned.

During the night, she dreamed about him, wanton and sweaty dreams of lovemaking that left her crying out with pleasure.

In each dream, he'd come to her wrapped in a pure white towel, and then he would let the towel slide to the ground with a sly smile on his face.

Chapter 7

For what seemed like the hundredth time, Aaliyah sighed and put the book back down on the night-stand. She was tired of reading and watching television. She'd even offered to help in the kitchen, but Mrs. Clarke had run her out of the room, making it clear she was a guest.

Picking up the book once more just to fling it back down with vehemence, she then stood. She was tired of Dominic's diva complex. She knew he was haunted by something from his past, but that was no excuse for taking time off from therapy. It was as if he didn't understand the importance of what she was doing. Based on her assessment, the progress he'd made in the short time since they'd started was positive. But if he chose not to continue, he would spend the rest of his life limping around the place with a hand that was barely functional. She'd met stubborn patients before, but Dominic Wolfe totally took the cake.

She had every intention of finding him and giving him a piece of her mind. She didn't care if he was her boss. She'd kept quiet for too long.

She put on her slippers and headed to the kitchen. Maybe Mrs. Clarke would know where he was.

The kitchen was empty. She groaned in frustration. Maybe he was in his room. She should have stopped there on her way down to the kitchen.

She ran back up the stairs, taking two steps at a time. When she reached his suite, she knocked but there was no response. Not allowing herself to be deterred, she pushed the door, watching as it swung open. She stepped inside, closing the door behind her. It was empty. She walked forward, wondering if he was in the bathroom, but she could not hear a sound.

He wasn't there.

She turned to leave when she heard a loud sound. She glanced in the direction of the noise and noticed a door to the left of the room. She walked slowly toward it, wondering what she'd find behind it.

For a moment, her hand hovered over the doorknob, but then she slowly turned it.

Her entrance was greeted with another noise. Dominic sat by a worktable, one for sculpting. Several misshaped lumps of clay lay on the bench while miscellaneous bits of clay lay scattered across the surface. She gasped. She'd interrupted his tirade.

He turned around.

"Are you ever going to stop intruding on my life?" he barked. She could see his embarrassment.

"I'm sorry. I needed to speak to you."

"For what reason?"

She couldn't believe he'd asked that question.

"I'm seriously beginning to wonder why I'm here."

"I hired you. I pay you," he snapped. "That's why you're here."

"But you're not letting me do my job. Every day there is another issue."

"I still can't see what the problem is. Even if I don't get therapy, you'll still get paid."

"Well, I'm not sure about the people you're accustomed to dealing with, but where I come from, we give an honest day's work. I can't continue to take your money if I don't work."

"You're strange," he replied.

"No, the word is honest."

"Well, I beg to differ."

For a moment there was silence. "So how is your hand coming along?"

"It's doing fine. Can't you see my handiwork?"

"I didn't know you could sculpt."

"As you can see, I'm not very good at it."

"With your hand as it is now, that would indeed be challenging." She glanced around the room, noticing a few finished pieces. "You did these before the accident?" she asked, pointing at no piece in particular. Though she immediately realized that she had asked a silly question.

"I completed a bit of my work in high school. My

teacher thought I was good, but the lure of the bright lights was a lot more appealing. My drama teacher thought I was talented, as well."

"So you chose the bright lights?"

"I did. And you don't have to say it with such disdain. I'm good...*was* good at what I did."

"I have no doubt you were, but playing an action hero isn't really proof of your ability to act."

She immediately realized that she'd said something she shouldn't have.

His eyes turned surprisingly sad.

Instinctively, she raced over to him, placing a hand on his shoulder. He stood slowly, the sadness in his eyes changing to pain.

They stared at each other, anticipation sizzling and tension crackling. Then she pulled him gently to her, placing her arms around him. His head dropped to her shoulder and rested there.

She raised a hand, placing it on his head as she touched him softly. His body tensed, coiling like a spring, and then he sighed softly. His body relaxed as if the pain he carried had left him. Inside she moaned, his closeness stirring something inside her she'd thought long buried.

She loved the feel of his body against her own. He was all hardness and male. She ached to run her hand against his firmness, to feel his warmth beneath her palms.

At that moment, he raised his head and looked her full in the eyes, as if to question what was happening between them. But she didn't want to think logically. She just wanted to feel.

She didn't give him an answer in words. Instead, she tilted her head upward, placing her lips on his. At first the kiss was a whisper, a soft feathery flicker, a tender connection of cautious lips.

He tasted her.

She tasted him, inhaling at the same time his musky earthy scent.

The pressure of the kiss increased, until his tongue slipped between her parted lips. She groaned with pleasure as heat coursed through her body. She shuddered. His body trembled in response.

She loved the feel of his tongue inside her, exploring, touching, caressing. She captured it, sucking deeply, until his body shivered again. She felt the first stir of his arousal against her leg. She reached down, cupping his hardness with her hand, smiling when it jerked with excitement.

Then he pulled away from her, ending her moment of awakening. Even now, she could still taste the sweetness of his lips.

"I'm sorry. I didn't mean for that to happen," she finally said.

"I take full blame for what happened. You offered me comfort and I took advantage of you. I promise it won't happen again."

His words drenched her in cold water, but she understood what he meant. Their relationship had to remain professional if she were to be successful with his recovery.

She'd also stepped over the boundaries.

"I agree. I'll make sure it doesn't happen again, sir."

"Well, since you came here to talk to me about my therapy, I promise you that starting tomorrow, I will be at all of my sessions."

She nodded. "I'm going to go back to my room."

With that, she turned to walk away. His voice followed her. "I did enjoy the kiss," he whispered.

She didn't look back, but for some strange reason, her heart felt light and carefree.

Dominic watched as Aaliyah walked away. He ached to call her back, to finish what they'd started. But he knew that would only complicate his already shaky relationship with her. But damn, she kissed so well. He could have spent the whole afternoon kissing her and still want more.

He closed his eyes, remembering the feel of her hands on him. When she'd cupped his penis, it had taken all his willpower to control himself. He'd been so close to losing control.

He sighed. For some reason, he was being noble. The Dominic of months ago would have taken her right then and there, without any reservations.

But he respected her. He liked her. While she did behave a bit too bossy for his liking, there was something about her that appealed to him.

Maybe it was her innocence and naivety. He kept saying that she was not his type, but on reflection, he wasn't even sure if he had a type.

He looked around the room, knowing he needed to clean up. It would take him a bit longer with one hand, but he'd get it done, as he always did.

He really needed to stop tossing the clay around in anger. He needed to take a close look at himself. He wasn't one to lose his temper. He'd always prided himself on the self-control he exhibited under pressure. The circumstances in his life had changed him and he didn't like what he saw.

When he'd finished cleaning the room, he headed outside. He hadn't spent any time with Nugget in the past day. He knew the puppy missed him. Nugget always missed him.

When he entered the kennels, he immediately went to Nugget's tiny compartment. The puppy barely raised his head. Instead, Nugget glanced at him with sad, disappointed eyes. The pup shifted his body and turned his tiny bottom in Dominic's direction.

Dominic chuckled. So Nugget wasn't going to be friendly.

He reached for the pup, taking him into his strong hand. Nugget wiggled his tail reluctantly.

"Okay, I'm sorry. I shouldn't have ignored you for the past day. I'm human. I was just dealing with some issues. But I promise it won't happen again. You want to go for a walk?"

The dog's tail wagged faster. He smiled. He'd been forgiven.

Half an hour later, he sat in his usual spot, looking out to sea. He loved it here on the cliff's edge. Above the waves, a white egret flew awkwardly, its large feet seeming to slow its movement. Despite this, it dived ungainly downward, eventually rising out of the water with its meal wiggling within its mouth.

He laughed out loud, something he hadn't done in months. He felt different, lighter. As expected, Aaliyah came to mind. She was taking over his being, tantalizing him with her proprietary behavior. At school, she would have been considered a good girl, and he a bad boy. They were the total opposites, from what he could see. But he could not deny his attraction to her, an attraction he didn't rightly understand.

In the distance, Nugget barked wildly. He'd found a crab.

Suddenly, the pup yelped and raced in Dominic's direction. Nugget then came to an abrupt stop, lying on the ground, his paws rubbing his nose.

Cautiously, Dominic kneeled down, tickling the pup's stomach. Nugget lifted his legs, closed his eyes and relished the attention, his painful encounter with the crab forgotten.

"You ready to go back home?"

Nugget stood and wagged his tail in agreement.

Forgetting his misadventure, the pup raced in the direction of the path that led to the house, stopping briefly to make sure Dominic was following.

It was that time of day he loved most—mealtime— and his excitement about eating never ceased to amuse Dominic. He could only think of very few things that didn't excite Nugget. The pup was a bundle of endless energy…. Well, most of the time. He quickly remembered the dog's reaction before their walk.

Tonight, he'd go back to the workshop and work on the sculpture he'd started this afternoon. He'd achieved some progress using his right hand, though at first it had felt awkward.

He reached the end of the path and headed to the kennels, where Nugget was already waiting patiently. He'd opened the nearby storage shed, quickly retrieving the smallest bag, which contained Nugget's chow. The older dogs had already been fed and lay lazily watching him with indifference.

"Have a good night, boy," he said, bending to rub the pup's tummy. Nugget yawned in response and then closed his eyes.

Dominic walked slowly to his room. He'd take a shower and then head to the workshop.

The next morning, Aaliyah watched as Dominic lifted the weight for a final set and then allowed it to drop with a bang. The tension in the room was evident.

He then rose from the bench with an energy she hadn't seen the whole morning in him.

"So why couldn't you have given me that kind of liveliness during our session? You know what? I'm tired of your attitude! There, I've said it. And I'm not sorry. I've worked with people whose challenges were worse than yours. They worked so hard the impossible happened. I know people don't believe in miracles. But I do. I've seen people who doctors say would never walk again creep, then crawl and then walk."

She paused for a moment, waiting for him to fire

her. But he said nothing, only looked at her with an expression of pure shock as he sat back on the bench.

"So you can sit here and decide what you want. And when you've decided, you can let me know because I have no intention of wasting my time on a man who doesn't even care if he gets better."

She walked to the door.

She turned and faced him one last time. "You know, if you want to heal, these sessions can't be about going through the motions. You have to fight. What disappoints me most is that you seem to want to give up without a fight. That's not the man I know that you are."

With that, she walked out and slammed the door.

Outside, she breathed deeply. She had no doubt that she'd get fired, but she didn't care. She'd said what he needed to hear. Hopefully, some of it had penetrated his thick skull. She'd met men in the past, her husband included, who were stubborn, but Dominic Wolfe, celebrity, model and actor, took the trophy.

Dominic watched as she walked out. The battle between them seemed unwilling to come to an end. He stood again, groaning at the pain that shot up his legs.

He exited the room, closing the door gently behind him, and headed to his room. He was pissed off. What gave her the right to talk to him like that? He was her boss and he was paying her an excessive sum to give him the best care and treatment. He should fire her and send her packing back to New York.

He paused. She was giving him the best of care,

he reasoned. He was the one behaving like an ass. From the time she'd come to the island, he'd put up barriers to frustrate her.

Did he really want to get better?

He lowered himself to the bed, realizing that he was still hot and sweaty from the session. He didn't care. The sheets could be changed and even replaced if he wanted.

He stared up at the ceiling fan swirling around him. A wave of sadness washed over him. Was this what he wanted for his life? An isolated life that left him feeling sad and alone? One of the dreadful things about coming here was the realization that those people he'd called friends were not really friends at all. Without blinking an eye, they'd deserted him. He had planned on denying them entry to the hospital. He didn't want them to see him in such bad shape. However, they'd never come. He'd realized at that time that despite his celebrity status, he'd been alone.

When he'd been discharged from the hospital, he'd run home to Barbados. Not that he could really call Barbados home. In fact, he'd never visited the island, not even when he'd purchased his house. His reason for buying it had been simple. He'd needed somewhere to come to when he'd wanted to get away from the craziness of New York and California, where his other homes were. Each time he'd attempted to come before, he'd recoiled at the decision.

At that time, coming back had scared him. He could not admit it to anyone, but he knew the memories of his childhood had been too strong.

But the accident and his recovery had changed that. When he'd stepped on the American Airlines flight that day, he'd tried to control the panic boiling inside as the island grew nearer and nearer.

The first few nights on the island, he'd hardly slept, expecting countless relatives to come visit unannounced.

Fortunately, those feelings had subsided and he'd settled into a comfortable existence.

But was that what he wanted? Or did he want to feel alive?

He closed his eyes, feeling the unfamiliar sting of tears. He didn't cry, not even when his mother had passed away.

But tonight, something strange was happening inside and he wasn't sure if he liked or wanted it. But the tears came, large wet drops that seemed not to want to stop. He gripped one of the pillows on his bed and buried his head in its depth.

When he was all cried out, he felt better. Felt as if a burden had been lifted off his shoulders.

For some reason, he believed that everything was going to be all right. Tomorrow would be another day, a different day. He didn't want to be sad and alone anymore. He wanted to live, wanted to be better, and the only way he was going to do it was if he felt like he was living.

He rose from the bed and walked to the bathroom. The usual pain was there, but it was slightly more bearable.

After taking a shower, he headed for his workshop.

For some reason, he felt inspired. Maybe he could get the project he wanted to work on started.

He sat on the stool with his gaze on the lump of clay lying there. He placed his hand on it, feeling its warmth radiate playfully under his fingers. He started tentatively, the awkwardness of using his left hand a hindrance at first, but he calmed himself, making sure to take his time. He raised his right hand, immediately feeling the pain, but he tried to ignore it. Sweat formed on his forehead and nose, dripping onto the worktable, but he fought through the pain until it became the usual irritating throb.

Under his hands the clay came alive, and the mound started to take shape and form. It was crude and imperfect, but the shape of the egret was clear. The wings spread wide hinted at the bird's awkward flight, but there was a sense of freedom that he'd wanted to achieve. He looked at his work and felt an overwhelming sense of satisfaction.

Unexpectedly, pain cramped his fingers, causing him to grunt. His hand tingled and throbbed. Maybe he'd done too much, but that did not lessen his sense of accomplishment.

He glanced at his cell phone. It was long past midnight. He didn't realize he'd worked so long. He was tired, but he did not feel like moving. His hand felt tired and sore.

He moved to the small couch against the wall. He'd rest for a few minutes, then head up to his room. He had therapy in the morning and he didn't want to be late.

Chapter 8

Aaliyah pushed the door of the workshop open. On the short couch, Dominic lay asleep, his feet hanging off the edge.

For a while she stood staring at him, unwilling to disturb his slumber.

In his dream world, he was different. While awake, there was a hardness about him; asleep there was a softness and gentleness she didn't quite associate with him. He looked incredibly handsome.

She walked toward the couch, coming to a stop and glancing down at him.

She called his name but there was no response. She reached down and shook him gently.

He slowly opened his eyes.

He stared at her; she stared back.

"I overslept, didn't I?" he asked.

"Yes, you did," she replied.

"I'm sorry. I really wanted to be there on time."

"That's fine. We can have our session later today. Change is good every now and then."

"You're sure about that?"

"Yes, I'm sure. I didn't sleep well last night, either, so I overslept, as well."

"I think I'm going to go up to my room, take a shower and get a few hours of sleep. You sure you'll be fine?"

"Yes, I have some work to do on my computer and I'd like to give my sister a call."

"Feel free to make any long-distance calls you want to. I'm sure you'd want to keep in contact with your family in New York."

"Thanks, I'd love to call my sister Eboni. It was hard to be separated from her again so soon, especially now that she is pregnant."

She noticed his puzzled expression.

"I have three sisters whom I was separated from when our parents died. Last year, the private investigator my sister Eboni hired found me."

"How old were you when you were separated?"

"I was fourteen. I'm the oldest. There's Eboni, then Keisha and Cindi. Eboni was ten, Cindi was eight and Keisha was seven when our parents died. Eboni and I have been trying to find our other two sisters."

"It may not be easy, but I'm sure you'll find them."

"Eboni has a lot more faith than I do. She keeps

saying that she knows we'll find them." She lowered herself to the couch.

"I would think you'd be the one with all the faith."

"I know what you mean. But it's different."

"I see no difference. You want me to be strong and have faith so that I can be whole again. It's the same type of faith."

She nodded in agreement. What he said was true.

"I remember when we were kids, our mother would read us fairy tales. I loved those stories, but always wondered why the characters were never like me. I realized that fairy tales were just what the name suggested. Tales…with unrealistic endings."

"You don't believe in happily ever after. I would think that most women do."

"I'm not sure I believe in endings like that anymore. Eboni still does. She got married last year to a wonderful man, she's pregnant and expecting her first child. So maybe she's living her fantasy, but she may be one of the rare ones."

"What's happened to you to make you so bitter?"

"I'm not bitter, but perhaps rather troubled by life. And you seem to be just as uneasy as I am."

"Maybe I am. I have reason to be. I've lost most of what made me into the person I am."

"But those are superficial things."

"I resent your calling my career superficial." Anger lit his eyes. "I loved my craft."

"So why all the action-filled testosterone flicks?" she asked.

"Just because I did those flicks didn't mean I didn't

want to do something else. I did a small indie project a few years ago and I was actually in negotiations to do something on a larger scale. From the time I read the script, I wanted the role. I appreciated the director taking a chance on me, and in the audition, I gave my all."

"So what happened?"

"I got the role and then this happened." He indicated his hand.

She nodded, feeling his pain. "I'm sorry."

"I don't want you to be sorry for me. I want you to continue to challenge me and push me to get better. I realize now that I've been really dumb. I'm definitely not the slacker type. I've always fought for what I've wanted."

She yawned.

"I think I need to get some breakfast and catch up on my sleep, and I see you need to get a bit of rest, too."

"I'm sorry. I didn't mean to yawn like that, but I am starting to feel a bit tired."

"I'll see you this afternoon. I think we both needed a break."

She watched as he rose from the couch. When she was sure he was safely up, she turned to walk away.

"Thank you," she heard him say.

She turned around.

"What for?"

"For making me want to live again."

Not knowing how to respond, she just smiled.

Maybe she'd done something right.

* * *

When Aaliyah arrived in the gym later that evening, she was surprised to find him there already. He wore an unexpected smile on his face. She'd never seen him smile during any of their sessions. In fact, he demonstrated total dislike for whatever took place in the gym.

"You're early," she said.

"I did promise you I'd be here."

He was dressed differently, less casual, as if he planned on taking his therapy seriously. She could not help but smile.

He smiled in return.

"So are you ready to get going?"

"Whenever you are," she replied.

"I'm ready."

That evening, she searched in the closet for one of two formal dresses she'd brought to the island with her. It was one of the dresses Cheryl had insisted she buy during her makeover.

She slipped it on, loving the feel of the fabric, just like she'd experienced the first time she put it on. She loved the softness of the blue. She glanced in the mirror, seeing the sexy woman who'd stared back at her just a few short weeks ago. Since arriving on the island, she'd buried that person in her old clothes, trying to make sure she looked professional.

Tonight, she felt soft and feminine. She felt strange. Even when Andrew was courting her, she'd never been really concerned about how she dressed. They'd known each other for so long, it hadn't seemed important. Their love was one that had grown over time.

She remembered her parents talking about their own love. Her parents' love for each other was not usual, but a special kind of love she didn't quite believe in. When she thought of love, she equated it with security and loyalty and commitments. Her parents shared the wild kind of love, controlled by emotion, that she had little time for.

She picked up her favorite fragrance, *Eternity Moments,* and squirted a bit behind her ears and other pulse points. She glanced in the mirror one last time. Content with what she saw, she headed downstairs.

When she entered the dining room, she was immediately greeted by the smooth sounds of Jill Scott's latest. She definitely had not seen Dominic as the jazz type, but it was a pleasant surprise.

He immediately turned. An unexpected grin lit up his face. Damn, he was gorgeous. She didn't usually think of men as gorgeous, but he was. Despite his attempt at a rugged look, he was clean shaven and his hair neatly cut.

He walked slowly toward her and she noticed his slight grimace of pain. She ached to comfort him, but she was his therapist. She had to try to remain professional, though that was becoming more and more difficult with each day.

There was a part of her that ached for more, that even now wished he would kiss her again and relieve the need she felt inside.

Breathing in deeply, she stepped forward, causing him to stop. She didn't want him to exert himself unnecessarily.

He paused by the table, waiting for her to reach him.

"Are you ready to eat or do you want to continue listening to some music?" The food was already there. She noticed the dishes on the buffet table, kept warm by the flickering flames of the sterno canisters.

"To be honest, I'd prefer to eat right now. My workout earlier has left me hungry and tired. We can listen to music while we eat."

"My sentiments exactly. I'm hungry, too. I haven't been eating much these days. I never was a big eater, but I haven't had much of an appetite since the accident."

"Well, let's see if we can improve your appetite tonight."

"Maybe." He pulled out a chair, indicating that she should sit.

"Thanks," she replied, lowering herself into the seat, but then rose again. "Remember, dinner is buffet-style."

"Oops, I forgot. Mrs. Clarke is off for the night. She has one of her never-ending church meetings."

"Do you want me to take care of your plate?" she said. "You just need to let me know what you want."

She immediately noticed his indecision. He was too proud.

"I'll get whatever you're having. Mrs. Clarke says they are all my favorites. So I'm sure I'll enjoy everything."

Aaliyah walked to the table, uncovering the dishes. Delicious aromas tickled her nostrils. Her stomach grumbled. She filled one plate with a selection and then the other.

When she was seated, she said, "Is that fine?"

"I thought you said you were hungry."

"I am hungry, but I think I've been doing a bit too much eating. Mrs. Clarke's cooking has been pure bliss, but I have to control my portions."

"I agree. I need to tone up a bit. Thanks to the sessions, I'm on my way back to a fit body."

Definitely fit, she thought. She would love to run her hands all over his tight, firm muscles.

"I must go to church with her while I'm here," she said, changing the conversation to a safer topic. "I don't usually miss worship on Sundays, but I wasn't sure about where to go while here. Do you go?"

"On occasion, but I haven't been since I came to the island. I haven't been feeling that sociable or spiritual," he confessed.

"It's in times like this, when you don't feel spiritual, that you need to exercise your faith."

"Well, my faith is a bit fragile right now," he replied.

She nodded. What he said was true. She remembered exactly how she'd felt when Andrew died. She'd not been in any way responsive to God. It had taken her a long time before she'd stepped back into church.

She picked up her fork, waiting for him to do the same. She tasted the first mouthful of creamed potatoes and sighed with delight.

"I didn't realize creamed potatoes could taste so good. Mrs. Clarke tempts me to always want seconds."

"I wasn't sure if I'd keep her on staff, but when I tasted her first meal, I hired her immediately. I just wish she were willing to travel, I'd take her wherever I go."

"I'm sure that when you travel, you eat."

"I do, but it's not the same as eating Mrs. Clarke's food. Definitely inferior. When I was in New York a few weeks ago, I couldn't wait until I got back home. I missed her cooking."

She lifted the fork to her mouth, tasting the succulent salmon, savored with the spices of the island.

For a while they ate in silence.

When she was done, she placed her fork down.

"Do you want dessert?"

"I'd just like a glass of wine, white preferably."

"I'm sure I can find a bottle or two. You want to retire to the living room? I'll go get a glass."

"I can get it," she offered.

"Just let me do it," he insisted. "I'm not totally helpless."

"I'll wait."

When he was gone, she turned the music up. Jill Scott's sultry voice came over the speaker system, which seemed to run through the whole house.

She stood, looking out the window, watching the dimming daylight and the first stars as they started to appear.

When he walked in, he carried a bottle of La Mondotte. She recognized it since it was Eboni's favorite wine. She'd always been content with the less expensive variety, but when she'd tried La Mondotte, she immediately tasted the difference.

He rested his cane against the wall and poured two glasses, handing her one when she reached him.

She took the glass and sipped daintily as she felt the warmth spread through her body.

She wasn't sure if it was really the wine or Dominic that caused the heat in her body, but she knew she liked being with him.

"I'm going to sit now. Sit next to me," she said.

He waited until she lowered herself to the couch before he sat next to her.

For a moment they sat in silence, savoring each other's presence.

"So how did you get into modeling and acting?" she asked, breaking the silence.

He hesitated for the briefest of moments.

"I was in high school and wanted to act, but not necessarily model. However, a woman, Chandra Crane, who owns the Crane Agency, saw me, liked my look and asked me if I were interested in modeling. Since I saw it as a stepping-stone to what I really wanted to do, and my father knew what I wanted, we signed the contract. I started modeling when I was still in high school. My first contract was with the Urban Boys clothing lines, and then I went on to bigger things."

"You grew up in New York?"

"Just my mid to late teenage years."

"Before then?"

"I grew up here."

"Here? In Barbados?"

He laughed at her excitement.

"Yes, here in Barbados. In fact, the village I grew up in is the one just beyond the trees at the back of the house. You can see the tops of the houses if you look closely."

"I didn't realize that. Do you still have family here?"

"No one I'm familiar with. That's the reason I moved to the U.S. When my mother died, there was no one to take care of me here. My father did the right thing and took responsibility for me. I didn't even know he existed."

"So how was it with him?"

"It was really fine. He was single, had money and was willing to give me whatever I wanted. Maybe to make up for the years he'd missed."

"So you like him?"

"Yes, I was sorry I didn't have more time with him, but the time I had was good. He was good to me. I loved him."

She thought briefly about what he said and then asked, "Why did you buy the house here?"

"I'm really not sure," he replied. "At the time, I was looking for a way to invest, and while I'd heard that land is pretty expensive here, I still thought it would be a good investment. When I saw that this house was going on sale, I decided to purchase it."

"You come here often."

"To be honest, the first time I came back to Barbados was just after the accident. My life has always been so busy and hectic. Though I did buy the place so I could have somewhere to come when I wanted a break from the craziness that's New York and L.A."

"You have homes there, too."

"I have a home in Scarsdale and I keep a condo in L.A."

"You have a home in Scarsdale? My brother-in-law, Darren, has a home there, too."

"Darren Grayson? I used his company when I purchased my U.S. homes. He's extremely wealthy."

"True, but despite that, he's pretty cool. You wouldn't believe he has all that money. Eboni is expecting their first child. I'll soon have my first niece or nephew. Though Darren does already have a little girl who is simple adorable, so technically speaking, I already have a niece."

"It must have been really exciting to find Eboni. I can hear the joy still in your voice."

"It was. When we all separated we promised each other we'd find each other, but as time went by, I thought to intrude on their lives might not have been a good thing. But Eboni was persistent. She's pretty well off, too, so she had funds of her own to hire an investigator."

"What does she do?"

"What do you mean?"

"Sorry, I meant her career."

"Now this is pretty crazy. She's a full-time firefighter and is a fitness trainer at a gym in Manhattan."

"Sounds interesting."

"Yes, from what she told me, her parents weren't too happy at first, but they love her. She could have followed in their footsteps as they wanted her to."

"In their footsteps?"

"Yes, they are both doctors and actually thinking about retiring."

"I don't know if I'd ever want to retire. I enjoy my work. Even now, not working has been driving me crazy. If this therapy doesn't work, I'll have to start thinking of alternatives to what I do."

"What about sculpting? You seem to enjoy that."

"I only see that as a hobby. I'm not sure I want to be one of those struggling artists. While I've earned and saved quite a lot of money, I'm sure that unless I continue to invest what I have I won't always have it."

She placed her glass down and stifled a slight yawn.

"I didn't realize I was boring you."

"You aren't, honestly. I'm just a bit tired. We did have a long day, especially after working out in the afternoon. I'll probably turn in early tonight."

"I'm going to do the same thing, but before you do I have something I want to show you."

"What's that?" she asked.

"Come. We have to go outside."

He rose from his seat, reached for his cane and walked onto the patio. She followed, waiting as he maneuvered the steps valiantly.

The lights on the grounds had been turned on, and what was a well-landscaped garden vibrant with color and life in the day was now a moonlit sanctuary. He walked her toward a tiny gate she'd noticed one day after she'd arrived on the island.

He reached into his pocket, took a key out and unlocked it.

He stepped back to allow her in and then followed.

The place was breathtaking.

In the middle of the secret garden was a small pool into which flowed a tiny waterfall, the gentle humming of the water soothing like a soft caress.

He placed his hand on her elbow, guiding her to a wooden bench on which an orange light lingered.

She didn't want to sit, content with absorbing the beauty around her.

"You like it?" he asked.

"I love it."

"It's one of the changes I made when I purchased the house. On one of my photo shoots, we used a garden which was pretty similar to this one, but on a smaller scale. Since I had the land, I wanted it to be something grand, but beautiful and serene."

"I could stay here all night."

"Unfortunately, the pool is not for swimming, but in the daytime, you'll be able to see the fish inside. I like aquariums, as you have noticed from inside the house."

"I'm going to sit and breathe in the atmosphere.... No, that's not the correct word. Ambience. Yes, that's the word I was looking for."

Aaliyah walked to the bench, hearing the tapping of his cane as he followed. As expected, he waited until she was seated before he lowered himself onto the bench.

"I love it here on the island," she sighed.

"I do, too. I didn't think I would. Too many bad memories from my childhood."

She didn't comment, waiting to see if he'd say more.

"One of the things that still remains in my memory is the gnawing, empty painful feeling you get when you're hungry. I loved my mom, but I could never understand how she allowed me to go hungry. She would have the money for rum and cigarettes and the unending parties she went to."

She could feel his pain, and the sting of tears moistened her eyes. She hurt for the little boy he had been. Her understanding of him was even clearer now and as she thought about him and what he had endured, she resolved to make sure that when she left the island, he was well on his way to recovery.

"Didn't your father know about you? What was happening?"

"My father knew nothing about me when he left the island. My mother got pregnant by him. And when his parents returned to the U.S., she discovered she was pregnant and did nothing to let him know.

"When she died, I wasn't even sure what would happen to me. And then out of the blue, a man I didn't know came for me and told me he was my father. I had no doubt he was my father. I was his spitting image. There I was, a scared fourteen-year-old teenager, and this big hunk of a man puts his arms around me and cries. I cried, too. From that day, he did all he could to make me happy. I've never been hungry a day since, unless I made the choice to be."

"It must feel good when you have all you want."

"To be honest, I'm not even sure anymore. This situation has made me think about what I had, what I have now and what I've wanted for so long. And you have, too."

"Me?"

"Yes, you. You've made me start thinking about my career. What's important in life, in my life?"

"And what's important?"

"I'm not sure yet. I know what used to be important. What's important to you?" he asked.

"Life, love, memories."

"Not the future?"

"Not really."

"But that may be a bad way to live. We can't live in the past."

"How can we live for the future when we really don't know what it holds for us? We could plan our lives meticulously and then the unexpected happens and all our plans were for nothing."

He thought for a while about what she said. "I don't know if I totally agree with you, but there is some reasoning behind your thinking."

"The night is so peaceful and quiet. It makes you forget the outside world. Even in Barbados, something bad may be about to happen."

"True, but something good may be about to happen, too."

She remained quiet, hearing the change in his voice to subtle seduction.

"I want to kiss you."

"I want you to kiss me," she responded.

She turned to face him.

He leaned forward, his lips brushing hers lightly.

She shivered, a chill washing over her body.

"I love the taste of your lips," he moaned into her mouth.

His lips brushed over hers softly. She parted her lips, eager to feel his tongue inside her mouth. He didn't oblige immediately, tracing his tongue in circles around her lips, increasing her ache for his intrusion. When he finally slipped his tongue between her lips, she groaned, her body shivering again with anticipation.

When his lips moved from her mouth, she felt disappointed, her body still aching for his taste.

Then she felt the weight of his hand on her breasts, cupping the left one with a firmness that shot warmth to the core of her being. One finger circled an already turgid nipple, causing the heat to intensify. Her body burned with a fire inside.

"Oh, that feels so good," she moaned.

"Feels good to me, too," he replied, his voice filled with his own pleasure.

His mouth rained kisses along the curve of her neck, stopping briefly to nip on her ear. Her body shook as flamed desire heated her to the core.

He shifted, and then grunted in pain.

She pulled back, immediately concerned.

"Are you okay?" she asked, but she could tell he was not fine.

"Your leg or hand?" she asked.

"Hand," he said between clenched teeth.

She reached for his hand, taking it gently in hers. He growled, but she disregarded him, firmly kneading the hand between her fingers.

She glanced at him, noticing the beads of sweat on his forehead. She could tell he was doing all he could to bear the pain.

Slowly, he started to breathe, his body relaxing, the muscles in his hand responding to her kneading.

In time, his eyes closed, and she wondered if he'd fallen asleep.

When she was sure she'd done enough, she stopped.

His eyes opened immediately, staring at her with a gratitude that he reinforced with an uncertain nod.

"Feel better?" she asked.

"Yes. I should be accustomed to this by now," he reasoned.

"You'll be fine. While it may be bothersome, it's evidence that your nerves are coming alive again," she said enthusiastically.

"That's all well and good, but I don't think there is anything as painful as those muscle spasms. I think I'll go to my room now. I've had enough drama for the day."

She stiffened, hurt at his words. So he thought she was drama? While the message she received may not have been his intention, she realized the implication for her.

"I think I should be heading to mine, too. I need to get some sleep."

"You go ahead. I'll sit here for a bit."

He wanted to be alone and she appreciated that, but she wished he'd wanted her to stay. She would have been able to offer him comfort.

She rose.

"Good night, Dominic."

"Good night, Aaliyah," he replied with a smile that didn't quite reach his eyes.

Before she left, she bent and kissed him softly on his lips.

With that, she walked away, refusing to turn back.

What the hell was happening to him? For the first few months he'd been on the island, he'd been content to be away from the outside world. In fact, he enjoyed being on his own most of the time. Strange, since most of time he'd reveled in the attention showered on him by his fans, especially the women.

And he'd had no problem with women. From the time he turned eighteen, there was no end to the women who wanted him, and he'd obliged them. On reflection, he realized that they had only provided sexual gratification. Nothing more, nothing less.

Tonight, the embarrassing situation with his hand had only proved to him that he wasn't ready for love or a relationship. In fact, he wasn't ready to have intimate contact with any woman. It hadn't even been his leg. Just his hand, his useless hand.

He rose from the bench, walking as fast as he could.

His leg hurt, but he didn't care. He just wanted to get to his room. Away from eyes that stared at him too much when they thought he wouldn't notice. He saw the pity in Mrs. Clarke's eyes and the other staff members.

He hated it.

Chapter 9

Dominic walked out of the gym. He knew that he'd been unwilling during the session, but he couldn't help himself. Last night had set him back. He'd been heading in the right direction with his attitude, but the debacle with his hand the night before had only proved that he was less of a man. Yes, he had all the right parts, but his leg and his hand served to show him that any hope of romance was only an illusion.

No woman would want a man in the position he was in. He couldn't imagine himself walking up the aisle with a cane in one hand. How the hell was he going to hold a ring?

"We're going down to the beach. You left before I could tell you," Aaliyah said, interrupting his thoughts.

"To the beach? I'm not sure if that's a good idea."

"It's really not what you think. I've been given the go-ahead to use the methods I see appropriate for your treatment and Dr. Graham has agreed about the beach therapy."

"You mean now?"

"Yes, that's why I cut this session short. You thought I was giving you the time off because you were a good boy?"

He grinned. He couldn't help it.

"I'm sorry. I didn't mean to be a jerk."

"Well, you were one. While I didn't expect our relationship to dramatically change, I really did expect you to be a lot more pleasant, Mr. Wolfe."

"So we're back to Mr. Wolfe?"

"I really wasn't sure. Is it Mr. Wolfe, or should I call you sir?"

"I was that bad?"

"Worse."

"When do we go to the beach? Now?"

"Yes, I'm just going to go upstairs and get what I need."

"I'll wait in the backyard for you. Can I bring Nugget?"

"Sure. But he'll have to stay out of the way."

"He won't be any trouble. As long as he sees a crab hole he'll be happy."

"Good. I'll be back."

When she disappeared, Dominic returned to the gym, searched for a loose-fitting pair of trunks and headed to the kennels for Nugget.

As he approached, the barking of delight started. He bent, patting the dog on his head, causing him to spin around in circles.

"Come. Let's go."

Nugget tore ahead of him, coming to a stop by the gate. When Dominic opened the gate, the dog raced outside, running around with an energy that could only be a result of him being confined for a few days. Vowing never to let it happen again, Dominic followed the dog down to the path that led to the beach.

Aaliyah was there waiting.

When he reached Aaliyah, she bent down to scratch the dog behind his ears. Nugget looked up at her with utter adoration.

He shook his head, wondering if he wasn't doing the same thing. He was convinced he was staring at her with his own look of admiration.

"Well, I'm ready. Lead the way and I'll follow. I hope the path to the beach isn't too rocky. I wouldn't want you to hurt your leg."

"I'll be fine," he replied. "I know this area like the back of my hand. There are steps going down to the beach. I've been down a few times. It wasn't easy, but I made it."

They walked along the cliff's face, watching Nugget's antics as he stopped to examine every hole he passed.

The trip down the steps leading to the hidden cove took longer than he'd expected, but part of the enjoyment was walking behind Aaliyah and admiring the nice curve of her behind.

The beach was empty. She'd noticed his sigh of relief when he saw that no one was there. He'd informed her that on the island, beaches could not be privately owned, a government policy.

She knew that people being around was one of the reasons he'd hesitated when she'd first asked. While Dominic was fit, his body well toned, his abs forming a solid six-pack, one leg was noticeably smaller than the other. But she'd already noticed the hint of rebuilding muscle tone. The few scars, a result of the accident and surgery, had faded and were hardly noticeable.

"We won't go in the water today. Just walk on the sand. Because the sand is soft, it'll force you to use your leg muscles even more. Ready to walk?"

"Not going in the water?" He folded his arms in defiance.

"We can walk a bit in the water, but I promise we'll go completely in next time. I just need to make sure your leg is strong enough."

After walking a few laps up and down the beach, she suggested they return to the house.

He stopped. "Do we have to leave now?" he asked. "We could chill on the beach for a bit. We don't have anything to do for the rest of the day."

"Where?"

"Over there," he replied, pointing out a row of almond trees.

She picked her gym bag up and wrapped a towel around her waist. She wished that Dominic would do the same thing. Since he'd taken off the shorts, the green-and-black close-fitting trunks did little to hide the generous bulge. Her eyes seemed to have a mind of their own, focused in on his crotch.

When he reached for his shorts and slipped them over the trunks, she sighed in relief.

She didn't want to spend the rest of their time on the beach having naughty thoughts.

When she reached the shade of the trees, he waited until she spread her towel down and then lowered herself onto it.

He lowered himself next to her, his leg brushing against hers. She looked at him; he looked at her. Heat sizzled.

At the same time, Nugget, who'd disappeared on one of his hunting trips, reappeared, plopping himself down. He stuck his tongue out and promptly closed his eyes.

"He's like a little kid," Aaliyah said, laughing.

"Yes, he is. When I went for a day not taking him out, he refused to acknowledge me. He made sure I knew he was displeased."

As if Nugget knew they were talking about him, his eyes peeped open. He looked at them solemnly and closed them again.

"I've learned my lesson," Dominic said. "It definitely won't happen again."

With eyes still closed, Nugget's tail thumped on the ground, causing sand to fly all around.

"I can tell you love it here."

"I do, I love the quiet. But I still miss New York. I love the energy of my job. I'm not sure if when I return I won't do things differently. But I know I've changed or should I say, I'm changing."

"I don't want to intrude, but could you tell me about the accident? What happened? I know you saved a little girl's life, but I'd like to hear it from you."

"You want to be my shrink now, too?" he replied.

She couldn't tell what he was thinking, but she didn't think he was annoyed.

"Lighten up," he said. "I don't like to talk about it much, but I want to tell you."

"Thanks. I don't want to be rude."

"You aren't. It's natural to want to know."

She nodded.

"It really wasn't that much. I was heading home from work one night when I saw smoke rising from a townhouse in a Brooklyn neighborhood. I pulled into a parking space on the other side of the road, crossed over and saw a little boy standing there looking through the open door. He told me his sister was inside and his mom had gone to the store to get pizza."

"She left them all alone."

"Yes, she sure did. But I'm sure he felt she'd be back real fast," he observed. "All I could think about was the little girl trapped inside. Without hesitation, I raced inside and climbed the stairs where her brother said she was. Fortunately, the flames were at the back of the house and I only had to worry about smoke. I didn't know that smoke could be so thick."

"You must have been scared."

"I was while I looked for her, but I finally found her. She ran into my arms, I lifted her and started to head back down the stairs. By then, the flames were swirling up the stairs and I had no idea what to do. I tried the other direction, not sure if there was a way out, and then the flooring collapsed."

"Oh, my God."

"When I landed, I tried to break her fall, and then the ceiling opened and everything came tumbling down. I was able to push her out of the way before anything fell on her. However, a large piece of furniture landed on my left side, trapping me with its weight. The little girl got out and told them where to find me. However, by the time they came for me, I was unconscious. My left side had been damaged, and here I am."

"But you saved the little girl's life."

"If I had to do it again, I'd still do it. The girl, Anna, came with her parents to visit me in the hospital. Despite this—" he indicated his hand "—I have no regrets doing what I did."

"I'm proud of you," she said.

He looked across at her. "It was nothing."

"That's your thinking, but I'm sure that little girl and her parents don't see it as nothing."

"I suppose."

She didn't push the issue. He clearly failed to see

that what he had done was a reflection of his nature, the person he was.

She glanced down at her watch. "It's getting late and I'm getting hungry." Ironically, his stomach took that precise moment to growl.

"Seems like you are, too." She giggled girlishly, getting to her feet and reaching her hand out to help him up.

He took her hand. The familiar heat caused her lips to go dry. Their eyes met. Then Nugget barked, and they both looked down.

The moment was lost, but they were both aware of the shimmering tension between them.

"Let's get to the house. I'm starving."

That night, after a quiet dinner in her room, Aaliyah exited the house, heading toward the secluded garden where she'd been with Dominic the night before.

She pushed the gate, entering cautiously, but there was no one there. She was glad to be alone.

What was happening? She'd come to the island for a new start, a new beginning, and instead she found herself experiencing feelings she was not sure she wanted. Was she falling in love or was it a mere attraction? Was she feeling sorry for him and his ordeal? Or was it more? All these questions bombarded her, but the answers didn't drop out of the sky when she looked upward. Instead, she saw thousands of stars twinkling.

Well, she was the one who wanted change, and that was exactly what she was getting.

But was she being disloyal to Andrew? He'd just passed away a few short years ago and here she was lusting after someone. A wave of guilt washed over her. Since Andrew's death, she'd felt no interest in anyone…until now.

Instead, she would lay awake at night, tossing and turning and thinking of Andrew's gentle lovemaking. He'd not been a passionate individual. Their love had been the quiet, gentle kind. That was what she'd needed at the time. She had no need to experience the wild emotion that took her breath way and made her ache all over.

Those were the type of feelings that led to mistakes and heartache. She didn't want that and that was what any involvement with Dominic would result in. He was her total opposite. He was intense, passionate and wild. She'd felt his intense energy in his kiss. She could only imagine what would happen if she were to make love with him.

He'd make love to her and then leave her wanting more…and more.

The hairs at her nape stood up. Her heart quickened its pace.

She felt him, even before he spoke.

"It's a beautiful night, isn't it? Besides an island sunset, there is nothing more majestic than a night like this. Crystal-clear moon and the freshness of an ocean breeze."

She didn't respond, wondering how such poetry could flow from his lips.

"I'm so sorry. I must have intruded on your quietude. I often come here when I want some peace and quiet myself."

"I can see why. I can feel the magic."

"You believe in magic?"

She thought about his question. "To be honest, I've never really thought about it. It's one of those things we say without even thinking about it."

"But it does have meaning. Maybe the two of us are too cynical to see the beauty of it. Maybe I came here searching for magic or what appears to be magic. Have I found it? I'm not sure, but there is something special about this place."

"I know what you mean," she replied. "Even I feel it."

"I feel it, too. Even what's between us feels magical."

"And crazy," she added. "And wild."

"You feel it, too?" he asked.

"I do." She paused. "But I'm not sure I want to feel it. Not right now. I'm not ready for this."

"But that's the magic of it. The unexpected, the awe and surprise."

"Times like this, I miss my husband most."

"I'm sorry. You must have loved him a lot."

"I did. He was my husband, but he was also my best friend. I met him when I was in foster care."

"No wonder this—" he pointed at himself "—worries you."

She did not respond.

"But you can't go on mourning him. I'm sure he would want you to be happy."

"I'm happy. Just not ready for involvement."

For a while the conversation halted and all she could hear was the whisper of the wind and the sound of her heartbeat.

She leaned over to kiss him, her lips touching him tentatively. At first, he remained still and unresponsive. She then deepened the kiss, noticing that he'd relaxed and pressed against her.

And then he pushed her away, startling her with his reaction.

"What's wrong?" she asked.

"This makes no sense to me. I'm not one for pity, and maybe that's the reason you kissed me. Especially after saying you don't have any need for me and that you still love your husband. So what's in all of this for me? Are you trying to make me feel that I'm still a man?"

"Why would you think that, Dominic?"

"Because who wants a cripple as their true love? I know my limitations. Don't know if I'd ever be good again."

"You're being ridiculous."

"Then I think it is best I bid you good night. I'm heading up to bed. You enjoy the rest of your night."

With that, he gave her a dull look and walked away.

She remained silent. A few minutes later, she heard Nugget's strident barking.

She sat there, her mind troubled by things she did not want to think about.

She did not realize at first, but tears had begun to trickle down her cheeks.

Chapter 10

The clock struck midnight and she placed the book down. She could not sleep. The situation with Dominic had been going so well, but she could not think of the logic of her rejection. She knew it was more than what he said, but she could not for the life of her think of what it was.

She rose from the bed, heading to the shower. While the windows were open, the usual chill from the ocean seemed still and unmoving.

She turned the shower tap on, almost screaming in shock at the coldness of the water, but she endured, hoping the chilled water would give her relief from the heat she was experiencing inside.

When she was done, she lay on the bed, channeling her thoughts to brighter things, but still Dominic's image came to mind.

She rose from the bed. She'd go to him. She needed to talk to him.

She walked swiftly along the corridor, her footsteps vibrating against the floor. She slowed her speed. She did not want to wake the whole household, but quickly remembered that Mrs. Clarke lived in the left wing of the house.

When she reached Dominic's room, she knocked quietly. There was no response. After a few minutes, she turned to walk away, but heard the turning of the lock.

She turned around and he was standing there. Her heart stopped.

She could not breathe.

He was wearing an open robe, the belt hanging down. Her gaze lowered to where glimpses of his hair twirled upward. The thought of what lay beyond stirred her and she nearly moaned with her arousal. He felt the same way. She could tell. His lips were slightly parted and his eyes, smoldering with heat, lowered to her breasts. They strained against the sheer material of her nightgown.

"What are you doing here?"

"You know," she replied, stepping boldly forward.

He did not move, only shifting the front of his gown to hide his arousal.

"What you said was not true. I miss my husband, but all I have are fond memories. I've been ready to move on for a while, but I've had no real reason to.

But you have changed all of that." She reached for his hand, placing his palm against the mound of her womanhood.

"Feel this. I feel something for you. I need to feel you."

Despite his arousal, he hesitated. A fact that disappointed her, but when he stepped forward, she sighed in relief.

She melted against him, loving his firm, hard body. She placed her hands against his chest, feeling the rapid beat of his heart. There was something unexpectedly calming and exciting about the pulsing underneath. She felt an unexpected connection to him.

She tilted her head upward, wanting to feel his lips on hers, taste the sweet power of his assault. He did not take long to oblige. His mouth covered hers, and immediately his tongue slipped between her lips, sending shivers of excitement down her spine and a molten heat through her body. She could feel the length and width of his penis against her stomach and she pressed herself further into him, wanting to feel his heat against her. His erection, long and hard, jerked against her and she giggled.

"What's so funny?" he asked.

"This," she replied, slipping her hand between the folds of his robe, under his boxers, and gripping him firmly, awed when it jerked in her hand.

This time she didn't laugh, her focus on the satiny texture in her hand. She stroked him, watching as his eyes closed and his nostrils flared. A rough groan escaped his lips and his hand covered hers, halting her caress.

"If you continue to do that..." He hesitated.

She smiled, not worried about what could happen. She just wanted something to happen. She felt wanton and bold, feelings she'd never experienced with Andrew.

"So do we stay here or do we go to the bed?" she asked.

He stared at her for a moment as if he wasn't sure who she was.

"While I don't have a problem with variety, with my hand in the condition it is in, the bed might be a better option. I would've loved to lift you up and take you there."

She could hear the disappointment in his voice, so she reached for his hand, willing him to follow her, titillated by the spark of fire from his touch. He complied, his own excitement evident by the painful arousal straining the confines of his boxers.

When they reached the bed, she turned to face him, needing the reassurance that they were doing the right thing. Desire flared in his eyes, and she slipped the nightgown off, allowing it to settle in a pool around her legs.

He followed suit, using his right hand to loosen the drawstring that kept his shorts up. Immediately they slithered to the ground. She helped him take his robe off, breathing in deeply as his penis rubbed against her.

She pressed herself against him, feeling the fullness of his erection and enjoying the fact that she'd aroused him.

"I want you to make love to me," she whispered into his ears. She was sure she sounded brazen, but she didn't care. All she wanted was to have him inside her.

"And *I* want you to make love to me," he echoed. She nodded in agreement, but then realized what he was saying. She instructed him to sit and he complied.

She moved him onto the bed, and he eased flat on his back. His penis, loosened from its constraints, stood erect. Flames, potent and hot, flared in his eyes.

When he pointed at the dresser, she was not sure what he meant, but then it dawned on her. She shifted off him briefly, searched the first drawer and immediately found the package of condoms. She opened the package and took one out. She then rolled it skillfully onto his thick length, aware of the groan of pleasure that left his lips and the sudden shudder racking his body.

When she was done, she gripped him firmly, feeling the warmth beneath her hands.

She moved onto the bed, straddling him, his eyes still focused on her. She took his penis in her hand guiding him inside her as she lowered her body onto him.

She eased down slowly, adjusting to his size. Eventually, her body relaxed and he stroked upward, impaling her completely with his shaft. Sweet pleasure coursed through her body and the flames inside her increased with intensity.

She moved up and down on him, eager to do most of the work. She didn't want him to be in pain. She felt strange, but there was a strange sense of power. She was in control.

When his length moved in and out of her, she felt immense pleasure. She contracted her muscles, feeling them grip him tighter, and listened to his loud cry of pleasure.

"I love this feeling inside you. You're so warm and tight, I feel as if I can't get enough of you."

"You like it," she moaned as she increased her pace, allowing him to move in and out of her, in and out, deeper, faster and firmer.

In response to his cries, she urged him on. "Deeper," she cried.

He obliged her. He moved his body upward, their bodies coming together with a frenzy he wanted to revel in.

Then a tingling of awareness began, the warmth rushing into the core of her being. When the orgasm hit her, she screamed loudly.

His body shuddered, while under her, his movement became erratic as he stroked upward until she felt the full length touch that very special spot. Her body tensed and as the pleasure of release came again, her moistness clenched around his manhood, giving him a release so intense, he screamed out, as well.

She collapsed on him, her body vibrating with liquid heat as wave after wave of pleasure coursed through her body.

When her breathing slowed, she shifted from atop him.

"I didn't hurt you, did I? I didn't want to be rough."

"I'm going to be fine." He kissed her on her forehead, reassuring her further. "That was incredible!" he said, a wide grin on his face.

"It was," she said. "It definitely was."

"So can we do it again?" he teased, his voice brimming with desire.

"Definitely. I just need to take a shower."

"So do I, but I'm not sure if I can move yet. I'm exhausted."

"Is your leg or hand hurting?"

"My leg slightly, though you did most of the work."

"I did, but you did make a worthwhile contribution." She reached down to grab his manhood, surprised that it was already hard again.

"Come take a shower with me, and then we can get some rest," she said.

"You sure that's a good idea? I'm already getting hard just thinking of making love to you in the shower."

"I'm sure you won't be ready yet."

"Want to bet on it?" he challenged.

Ten minutes later, her loud screams of release were enough to prove that she was wrong.

Chapter 11

The next week was filled with therapy and lovemaking, though thinking about ways he couldn't hurt himself were becoming a bit of a challenge. But their lovemaking appeared to be the perfect medicine for his healing.

In just a few days she'd noticed an improvement in his hand and leg. Fingers that once refused to bend now made the slightest of movement. Along with that, he was moving easier and with less pain.

The first time he'd noticed the change, his eyes had opened wide in awe. He'd said nothing else, just made sure he'd worked harder the next day.

She'd continued to work him hard during their sessions and then again at night when their passions soared to the heavens and their screams of ecstasy filled the room.

What she liked most were the times after their lovemaking when he'd hold her close as if he was scared to let her go. But in the back of her mind, she was still worried. Where was all this going to lead? Was this relationship just to last the length of her time there? Were they just friends with benefits?

In the early hours of the morning, these were the thoughts that troubled her as she lay next to him while he slept.

"Let's have one session on the beach today. This time, we're going into the water."

"Can't we use the pool? I know I haven't used it since I've been here, but it might be safer since you haven't been in the water yet. I can get Desmond to fill it up."

"That's fine, but the ocean is better. The movement of the waves is what we need."

He hesitated. "If you think that it's better, then I'm all for it."

His expression didn't reflect his response, but she chose to ignore it. She needed to get him into the water. He'd be amazed at its therapeutic effect.

An hour later, they reached the bottom of the cobblestone steps.

Aaliyah immediately took her shoes off, enjoying the feel of the sand underneath her feet. The golden sand was hard and firm. Closer to the water's edge, walking would be more difficult, but getting him to walk on the soft sand would help strengthen his leg.

Nugget barked, having arrived on the beach before they did. He'd raced ahead, his excitement eliciting laugher from both of them.

"Come," he said. "There's an area just a hundred meters down which is better for swimming."

She nodded in acknowledgement and followed him, admiring his improving gait. He was really doing much better.

When they reached the spot he'd indicated, she placed the bag that contained a few pieces of equipment and two towels on the sand. She removed the towels and spread them on the ground, then slipped out of her jeans and tube top to reveal a white bikini.

Even though he'd seen her naked, he was amazed by his response to her. His gaze lingered on her breasts. They were just how he liked them. Just the perfect size to cup with his hand, and her nipples were so firm he was getting hard thinking about them.

"I'm going into the water," he said.

"Not yet," she shouted. "We're going to walk on the sand for a bit to loosen the muscles, then into the water."

"But we walked down the hill."

"Yes, but that's a different kind of exercise. We need to loosen your muscles in preparation for the swim. Your muscles are getting stronger, but there is a definite possibility of cramping if you don't prepare yourself well."

"No problem," he responded. "You're the therapist. I bow to your wish." He lowered his head.

She laughed. "You're in a jolly mood today," she observed.

"Indeed I am," he replied coyly.

She laughed. "I'll get you for that later."

"I look forward to whatever punishment you have planned. I didn't know you were so kinky."

She punched him in the chest and he fell to the ground.

She lowered herself to the ground. "I'm so sorry, I didn't mean to hurt you."

His arm snaked from his side and pulled her head downward. The kiss was raw and firm, stirring up memories of their lovemaking.

His lips suckled on her bottom lip, while his hand caressed the curvy lines along her spine.

In the distance there was laughter, and he lifted his head. A group of boys were walking by.

"Ignore us," one boy shouted. "Ain't no problem with having fun."

"You just want to watch, you pervert," another one replied.

The boys' raucous laughter followed them down the beach, where they finally came to a stop, and leaped into the water with more fanfare than necessary.

"Since we have company, I promise I will continue my seduction later."

"So that's what it was? Seduction?"

"Now you're insulting me, honey." He feigned hurt. "I am sure if those boys had not passed by at that time, I would have been inside you, making you beg for release."

She could not respond. The image in her mind only proved to be motivation.

"I think we need to start those warm-ups and then off into the water."

He stood reluctantly, his mouth pouting.

She laughed.

"Let's get this over with so I can have some fun."

"Good. I was hoping we could start soon. I have something to finish at home."

She had no doubt what he meant. Her face lit up with excitement.

She rose from where she sat next to him.

"Yes, let's begin!"

Dominic strolled out of the water. He'd had enough. While he liked the water and had been an excellent swimmer, his arms were tired. Even still, he felt powerful and strong, almost invincible. He was healing. He could feel it in every fiber of his body, every sinew of muscle he had. For a long time the light at the end of the tunnel had seemed far away. In fact, there was a time when he'd felt that there was no light. But now he felt different. He stopped and lowered himself to the sand. He glanced to where Aaliyah still floated. Her body bobbed up and down, like the buoys that dotted the water.

Just beyond where she was, the group of boys amused themselves with dives and flips. He'd laughed at their exuberance. Their youthful vibrancy took him back to a time when he'd been one of the boys and his friends from the village would come to this exact spot on the weekends. Back then, this was the one place where he could be absolutely carefree. The other boys would bring food, and it was his responsibility to bring coconuts. He'd known the boys had given him the choice because they'd realized he never had money.

Adrian had been the one to have his back. He'd not thought of his childhood friend for ages. He'd been determined to place his past where it belonged…in the past, and Adrian was a reminder of that past.

Suddenly, a familiar scream jolted him from his thoughts.

He jumped up from the ground, buckling over in pain. He quickly straightened up, ignoring the throbbing at his side. He searched the sea frantically, trying to find Aaliyah, but he could not find the white of her swimsuit.

Instead, all he saw was a large wave heading toward the beach.

In the distance he heard the shouts of a boy. "She's over there."

His gaze followed the boy's pointed hand, immediately seeing Aaliyah, her hands flaying in the air. He hobbled across the sand, the stab of pain racing along his leg, but he continued.

By the time he reached the water's edge, three of the boys were holding Aaliyah and hauling her to shore.

Two of the boys raced over to where he stood.

"You okay, mister?"

"I'm okay," he replied.

"We're glad we were here. We've seen you around and know your legs don't work too well."

"Thanks, I'm glad you were here, too."

"No problem, big man. Glad we could help."

By this time, the other boys had helped Aaliyah to her feet.

"We'll go with you to the house," one of the boys said. Dominic glanced at him. The boy wore brown shorts and looked vaguely familiar. He wondered if the boy was related to someone in his village.

"No need to look at us like that. We ain't going to rob you," the boy said.

"No, that didn't even cross my mind. I'd really appreciate the help."

He turned to Aaliyah, who with the help of the boys, lowered herself on a shirt one of the boys had placed on the sand.

"I'll be all right," she said, followed by a fit of coughing.

"Maybe I should take you to the hospital?" he suggested.

"I don't think that's necessary."

"Then I'll call the doctor."

She opened her mouth to protest.

"Either you let the doctor come or I'm taking you to the hospital. You got a bad battering. Humor me. I want to be on the safe side."

She stared back at him, her eyes flashing with defiance, but when she spoke her voice was calm and controlled.

"Okay, but only because you insisted."

He smiled. "Good, I didn't expect to win that battle so easily."

"Okay, boys, I need you to help me take her up to the house."

"No problem." The boy with brown shorts complied.

"We'll get a chance to see the house," the tallest of the boys said.

"Oh, so you want to see the house?" Dominic asked.

"Yes, I'm going to own a house like that one day," the boy replied. The others nodded.

"It's always good to have dreams." The boy's words echoed so many of his at that same age. "I need one of you to go get my cane and the clothes over there. I'm going to let Aaliyah sit here for a while before we go back to the house."

Before he could finish, one of the boys raced over and returned with the clothes.

"Thanks," he said.

"We'll go back into the water. When you're ready to go, just give us a shout."

"Thanks," Dominic replied. "That's fine. You go enjoy yourselves."

With that, he took the beach towel the boy had retrieved and placed it on the ground.

Aaliyah shifted onto the towel, holding the boy's

shirt in her hand and asked, "I'm not sure whose shirt this is, but I'd prefer to wash it before I return it."

"It is fine, miss," the tall boy said. "Brandon has a washing machine at home. But I know he is not going to want to part with that shirt." He lowered his voice to a whisper. "His dad passed away a few years ago and it belonged to him."

"I'm sorry to hear that," Dominic said.

"That's fine, sir. He's fine. It's been a long time. He just loved that shirt."

At the same time, Brandon returned with his cane.

"You're from the village?" Dominic asked.

"Yeah."

"I was born there, too."

"I know." The boy's words surprised him.

"You do?"

"Yes, my dad told me about you. I recognized you the first time I saw you walking on the cliffs."

"Your dad?"

"Yeah, my dad was Adrian Keith-Roy Johnson."

Dominic didn't know what to say.

"He talked about you a lot. Took me to see all of your movies and boasted that he was your best friend when you lived in the village. Of course, I thought he was kidding me, until he showed me photos of you and him."

Again, he was at a loss for words.

"He always told me you'd come back to Barbados someday. But I'm sure he would have never thought you'd come to live here. I'm sorry you didn't come before he died."

Dominic could feel the sting of tears, but he fought them back. Instead, he felt anger at himself. Anger that he'd never see his best friend again. When he'd made it big he could have returned home. Maybe with all the money he had he could have helped his friend.

"Your mother?" he asked.

"She died when I was born."

"So who's taking care of you?"

"There's only Mama, but she takes good care of me. She's getting old, but she still thinks she can do all the things she did before. I do most of the stuff and make her think she's doing it."

At the same time, the other boys came running up. "We're hungry, so we'll go."

"Thanks, boys, but I'm feeling much better."

"That's fine," Brandon said. "We promised we'll walk you home to make sure you're both okay. We're ready when you are."

They walked slowly up the pathway and across the field to the house. The boys kept up a lively exchange of jokes and ribbing.

On the walk up, he noticed Aaliyah was quieter than usual. Since they'd fished her out of the sea, he'd been worried. The expression on her face reminded him of the little girl he'd saved. While he'd saved her, he knew it had taken her several months before she could sleep a whole night without waking up to the nightmare of flames around her.

He felt the unexpected desire to bring Aaliyah into his arms and comfort her.

When they reached the back gate of the house, he thanked the boys as they walked away.

"Brandon?" he called.

The boy looked back. "Just a minute. I want to ask you something."

The boy came back, curiosity in his eyes.

"I just wanted to let you know you can drop by here any time you want."

"Thank you, sir. I'd like that."

He gave the boy his number, hoping Brandon would remember, and waved him off.

"He seems like a good boy. It's hard losing both your mother and father at such a young age."

"I'm sure," he replied. He turned to face her. "You're sure you're feeling better?"

"I am, but I do have a slight headache."

"I'm calling the doctor as soon as I get in the house."

When the doctor arrived an hour later, the consensus was that Aaliyah would be fine. Dr. Brown had given her some pills to help with the slight pounding in her head and made her promise to retire for the day. Aaliyah had immediately headed to her room, leaving Dominic all by himself and…lonely.

It was still quite early, but for the first time since he'd moved to the island, he felt alive. He headed for his bedroom and went straight to the bathroom, deciding to take a long soak in the tub. It was strange how people built bathrooms with showers and tubs and rarely took the time to enjoy them. He stripped his clothes off and turned the faucet on, and decided to shave before he took the bath.

He got his shaving set from the cabinet beyond the mirror at the sink and proceeded to shave.

The task took him a bit longer than normal, but when he was done he glanced at his face in the mirror. While his face was not a replica of what the public saw in magazines and on the big screen, what he saw looked better than the image he'd seen for the past few months. It was not only the outer facade that looked different. His eyes no longer seemed dull and uninterested. What he saw now was a glimmer of the hope he hadn't dared to embrace.

He placed the shaver down and stepped into the tub, slowly lowering himself into the warm water.

He reached for the plastic bottle of soap and squeezed the floral-scented liquid into the tub. He was feeling happy. Meeting Brandon had been the highlight of his day. He'd cared about Adrian, and for a moment, a wave of sadness washed over him. One of the highlights of his days as a teenager had been his days with Brandon's father. His best friend had had the same sense of adventure as Dominic. Since he'd returned he'd tried to keep thoughts of his childhood friend at bay. He'd thought briefly about going to the village and asking around, but he'd not wanted anyone to see him as he was. He wanted their image of him to be the celebrity, not the poor boy who had made it out of the village. He definitely didn't want them to see his current pale reflection of himself.

He would go and check in on Aaliyah before he

went to bed. He still had to go down for dinner, but the throbbing on his side reminded him of the day he'd had. He was hungry. The exercise and the day had taken a toll on his body. While Aaliyah had come out of the ordeal unscathed, his part, or lack thereof, in the whole event had left him feeling useless. What would have happened if those boys had not been there?

He didn't even want to think of it. While he could do supervised exercises in the water, his ability to swim for an extended period of time was definitely questionable.

He wanted to see her, needed to see her. He rose from the water, unplugging the drain so the tub could empty.

When that was done, he dried and donned a pair of shorts and a polo shirt.

He exited his room and walked along the hallway to Aaliyah's room, his cane tapping on the floor. When he stood by the door, he raised his hand and knocked.

There was no response. He knocked a second time.

"Come in." Good, she was not asleep.

He pushed the door open and entered.

She was sitting up, her head resting on a large pillow.

She smiled briefly, grimacing with the effort.

"Do you still have the headache?"

"I was fine when I took the first pill, but I suspect it's time to take another."

Dominic glanced around the room, his gaze landing on the pitcher and glass on a tray on the dresser.

"Which of these tablets are you to take?" he asked.

"I have to take one of each just before I go to bed."

"I'll bring the cup of water to you." He walked over to the dresser, poured the water and picked up the tablets and handed them to her. "Did Mrs. Clarke bring your dinner?"

"I told her I wasn't hungry, but she insisted I eat some vegetable soup. I was glad she insisted. The soup definitely made me feel better."

"She cooks better than some chefs in many of the restaurants I've been to."

"Yes, she's a gem. I love her food. Especially the dishes from the island she makes. But she can cook those just as well as she can do everything else. I love the crab chowder she made the other night."

"That's one of my favorite dishes. She does it at least once every week. But I just came to find out how you were doing. I'll be heading back to my room."

She didn't respond immediately and he wondered why.

"You can stay if you want," she finally said.

His heart soared. He wanted to stay with her.

"I was hoping you'd ask, but I knew you may be tired and want to sleep alone."

"I don't like to sleep alone. I want you to stay."

"I'm already feeling tired. I've had my bath, so all I have to do now is hop in bed."

She smiled.

He crawled onto the bed, his side barely touching

her. She drew nearer and placed her head against his shoulder.

They both stared at the ceiling.

"Today was an interesting day," she said, breaking the silence.

"Yes, it was," he replied. "I need to tell you how sorry I am that I couldn't help you."

"I'm your therapist, Dominic. I know about your injuries."

"But what if the boys hadn't been there?"

"Let's not deal with what could have happened. The fact is they were there. But I'm positive that if they were not there, you would have reached me. You're stubborn and determined."

He didn't know what to say. She was a truly amazing woman. With a few simple words, she'd made him feel as if he'd been the one to rescue her, and she was right. He would have done whatever he could to get her out.

"I'm sorry about your friend," she said. "He died so young."

"Yeah, it's sad. I didn't even make an attempt to contact him when I left. He was my best friend. I don't even know how he died. I could have helped him."

"Maybe you can ask Brandon. I'm sure he'd tell you. He seems like a nice boy. Hopefully, he'll stay that way."

"I sure hope so. With the drugs and influences he probably has, it's going to be a close call. Even back then, when I was a kid, his father and I made the choice to stay away from those things. I hope Brandon did."

"So what are you going to do about the boy?"

"I know I have to do something. He's my best friend's son."

"I'm sure you'll think of something." She yawned.

"Are you feeling sleepy, like I am?" he asked.

"Yes."

"Then let's get some sleep. I can barely keep my eyes open." His yawn echoed hers.

"Me, either." She giggled.

Dominic turned slowly on to his side and used his hand to draw her to him. She curled her body into him, wanting to be close to him.

He smiled in the darkness. He'd always found images of couples lying the way they were so romantic. He felt that way right now.

A soft snore escaped Aaliyah's lips. It was sort of cute the way she snuggled up to him, a hand resting on the curve of his behind.

What the hell was going on with him? He was being all romantic. It just wasn't him.

Or was it? In the past, his focus had been on his career. He'd had no time for love or romance. In fact, he wasn't even sure if those things existed, especially for him. He had the occasional exclusive companion, but he had no problem moving on after things came to an inevitable end.

With Aaliyah, it felt different. She was different. From the time she'd stepped out of the car when she'd first arrived from the airport, he'd noticed the way she carried herself. There was an innocence and vulner-ability about her that made him think about her long into the early hours of morning. Despite those traits, she was sexy. It was not that bold, blatant sexuality he saw in the women who were part of his celebrity lifestyle. It was a sexiness that came out of not know-ing that you were sexy.

His thoughts about her were becoming crazier with each day.

Time for him to go to sleep and see what tomorrow would bring. Now he was looking forward to each day and what it brought him. He couldn't imagine his life without Aaliyah. Even the thought that he could have lost her today made him sad.

He moved his neck from side to side, feeling the weariness of the day resting on his shoulders. He needed to sleep. He raised himself on an elbow and kissed her on the cheek.

Closing his eyes, he was soon fast asleep.

In the middle of the night, he woke to the sound of rain hammering against the roof. He'd grown ac-customed to the sound. The rain had been active in recent months, a reflection of the season.

He'd never adjusted to the four seasons in the U.S. Here it was only the dry and the rainy season. He loved them both, but there was something about the time when the rains came that he found more appeal-ing. It was the time when the sugar canes swelled with intake of water, which was necessary to create the sweet liquid needed to make sugar.

Those were the nights, like tonight, were he would sleep with his window wide open. The ocean breeze caressed him with its gentle hands, until he would sleep like a baby.

Next to him, Aaliyah stirred and he looked over, only to find her eyes wide and staring at him.

"I want you."

"I may hurt you," he replied.

"You won't. I'm not some fragile porcelain doll."

To demonstrate how she was feeling, she raised herself on her elbows and moved herself above him. He gazed up at her, searching for the need for him in her eyes. He reached up, gently pulling her head downward, claiming her lips. He crushed her to him, her breasts against him. His tongue traced the softness of her lips and she responded freely to the shiver that raced through her body.

He slipped his tongue inside her mouth, kissing her with a hunger he could not understand. All he wanted to do was taste her sweetness, feel her trembling with passion.

His lips left hers to nibble gently on her earlobe. She shivered again and he trailed his lips along the curve of her neck, to the soft hollow by her shoulders.

He did not stop there, shifting his position so he could plant kisses at the curve of her breast. His tongue caressed a swollen nipple, before he covered it with his lips, suckling firmly until she writhed. He shifted to the other nipple, showering it with equal attention.

When he was done, he moved even lower, his

mouth tracing a line down her taut stomach until he reached the soft down between her legs.

She shifted slightly, her legs widening with welcome. He inhaled deeply, the still-lingering scent of her bath soap tantalizing him. When his tongue probed her entrance, she moaned hoarsely, her hand gripping his head and drawing him deeper inside.

He pushed his tongue inside, finding the firm nub. He flicked his tongue against it, tasting the sweetness of her honey and wishing he could taste her without stopping.

"I need you inside me," she whispered.

He withdrew his tongue, moving upward to capture her lips again. He plundered, devouring her softness, stirring when she responded with the same abandonment.

When their kisses no longer eased the need inside him, he shifted beneath her, reaching for a condom in the chest next to the bed.

When he moved toward her, she reached for the condom, taking it from him. He complied, knowing that she'd put it on with less effort.

He watched as she took it from the foil packaging, his penis jerking in anticipation. She laughed.

She reached for his hardness, rolling the condom onto it gently, laughing again when it jerked in her hand.

He didn't feel like laughing. His body burned like a furnace. He wanted to shout out loud, scream at the top of his voice, but he was sure the whole house would hear his cry.

Lying on his back made him feel open and vulnerable, his throbbing penis standing erect and straight. He started to shift his body, waiting for her to move over him.

She startled him when she pushed him back onto the bed.

She raised herself above him, holding on to his hardness before she slipped on to him, her muscles immediately clenching and releasing him.

When he was all the way inside her, she started a firm strong movement, her body going up and down on him.

There was something purely erotic about her movement and he felt his erection harden even more inside her.

Inside, the pressure continued to build and he moaned and groaned with the pleasure heating his body.

Raising his hand, he stopped her, watching as she paused momentarily. She rolled off him, lying on her back as she waited for him to shift position. He raised himself over her, placing himself in a kneeling position, which felt comfortable, and pulled her between his legs, her legs straddling his buttocks.

He eased himself inside her, but she moved forward, forcing him deep inside her. He gasped with the wave of energy that flowed through him.

Then he started to stroke, easing himself in and out, the sleek moistness of her vagina sending pleasure and pain along the length of his penis. She moved with him, enjoying the feel of him deep inside her.

Aaliyah felt the sweet pressure build inside her and felt Dominic increase his pace, thrusting into her with a deep, strong stroke. She reveled in the power and fullness of each stroke.

"I love being inside you," he groaned. "You are so tight and wet."

Aaliyah felt her body tighten, knowing her release was near. When he tensed and groaned deeply, she joined him as he shouted his release.

She drew him closer as he trembled and shivered on top of her, hearing his words of love. She held him tight, not wanting to let him go. She wanted to feel him near, to still feel him inside her. When he tried to shift his body off her, she tightened her arms around him.

"Don't move," she pleaded. "I want to feel you close to me."

Soon his breathing slowed and she realized he'd fallen asleep.

"I love you," she whispered into the silence.

Chapter 12

Aaliyah shifted slowly from the world of dreams and fantasy, realizing Dominic was no longer beside her.

Movement caused some discomfort, but it was definitely not like yesterday. There was only the slightest throb at her temple, but nothing she could not bear. She could take the medication as the doctor had recommended, but she hated any form of drug use. Over the years, and especially when she lived in the home, she'd seen the effect of drug use on others.

She could have easily been one of those kids, but her dream of being reunited with her sisters had kept her focused. Andrew, too, had convinced her that they had to make something of their lives.

Before she rose from the bed, she sent a silent prayer upward thanking God for sparing her life and promising that she'd do a better job of getting to church now that she was on the island.

Aaliyah decided she would cancel Dominic's session today and spend it relaxing in bed, as he'd suggested yesterday. She definitely didn't think she could work today.

She walked to the bathroom quickly, taking care of her daily routine and headed downstairs for breakfast. No one was there, so she ate quickly and then went in search of Dominic. She suspected he was in the workshop, so she headed there.

She walked slowly into the room, coming to stop just before him. He was so committed to what he was doing he had not heard her enter.

He was using both hands, his injured one moving slower, but he was beginning to use it more.

Tears sprang to her eyes. She knew that he must be in some kind of pain, but knew that with his newfound determination, he would work through it as he was doing now. She just needed to caution him to take it easy.

At times, he breathed deeply, his frustration evident, but he calmed himself, taking control, until the clay under his hands started to take shape.

He worked for a bit longer, and then stopped.

He immediately turned around. "Sorry, hon," he said. "I didn't want to stop until I was done."

"That's fine. It's good to see you using both hands."

"I've been trying. It's a bit uncomfortable, but I manage it."

"Just don't overdo it."

"I won't. In fact, that's why I stopped. I think that's enough for the day."

"So what are our plans for the rest of the day?"

"Want to go for a walk along the cliff?"

"That's fine. I'm sure Nugget would love that."

"Yeah, I was planning on taking the little guy along. Just let me clean myself up and I'll be down."

"I'll go get Nugget and meet you."

When they exited the room, she headed toward the kennels.

When she got to the kennels, Nugget was biting on a toy bone. Upon hearing her footsteps, he immediately looked up. The expression of concentration on his face turned to glee and he rose and raced to her.

"You want to go walking, boy?"

He yelped and wagged his tail in confirmation.

She opened the gate and let him out. Outside, he stood before her, his tail going at an even faster pace. As always, she could see his excitement. When Nugget saw Dominic, he raced toward him, unable to contain his adoration.

He barked and circled his legs until, tired from his exertions, he flopped to the ground.

"You're tired already? I'm going to have to put you back in your kennel."

As if understanding his words, the pup turned and headed for the gate.

Aaliyah and Dominic laughed, following an exuberant Nugget.

"He's something else," Dominic said. "He has a mind of his own."

They had reached the path that led to the cliff and eventually to the rock where she'd seen him sitting that first day.

Nugget was waiting patiently on them, his eyes focused on the wide expanse of space for his recreation. He gave an eager yelp.

"Go ahead," Dominic shouted.

Nugget didn't have to be told twice. With the speed of lightning he sprinted across the rocky surface, stopping abruptly at a crab's hole and waiting.

"The crabs are probably already shivering in their shells," Aaliyah said.

Dominic laughed in response. "Can't understand the attraction, but he'd be happy to sit there for the next couple of hours and crab hunt despite his last encounter."

"He must be a glutton for punishment, or he's working on his battle plan."

They walked over to one of the few almond trees that dotted the landscape.

Two large boulders of limestone offered them nature's seats. Aaliyah sat and Dominic lowered himself next to her.

The earthy, woodsy scent of his cologne wafted through the air, making her even more aware of his impact on her. She inhaled deeply. She loved the scent. It was strong and manly…just like him. He tried so hard to live up to his celebrity image, but she'd caught a glimpse of the man behind the facade. While the accident had left him uncertain and vulnerable, she could tell that this time in his life would be significant in determining the man he would later be.

"What are you thinking about?" he asked.

"About you," she replied.

"About me?" A strange look flashed across his face.

"Yes, you."

"You should really leave your thoughts for more pleasant things. I'm just a worn-out shell of a man who's reached the end too early."

"But you are so much more," she emphasized.

"I am? When I look back at my life for the past ten years, the only thing I've done that I can really be proud of is saving that little girl's life. Everything else was selfish and about me."

"But you did so much before. Movie stars work hard and while their work is confined to a two-hour movie, during that time, some of us get the chance to forget the outside world and be transported to a world that we enjoy."

"I've never thought of it like that."

"Maybe I haven't, either. I looked at the work you did and belittled it, but the reality is that the world is made up of diverse individuals with different dreams and ideas."

Overhead, an aircraft flew by, its noise drowning out the sound of her voice. She paused, looking up as the airplane moved farther and farther away.

"When I was a little boy, I used to come up here. I would sit under a tree and watch the airplanes rise into the air as they took off. I would dream of getting on one of those aircrafts and flying as far away from the island as I could."

"You did?"

"Yes, I did, but I never thought it would happen. I never thought my mom would die so young. But most of all, I never thought I would be on the cover of the most important magazines all over the world."

He paused.

"Do you believe it? This poor boy from that village just beyond those trees has enough money to buy that village and everything in it."

"You should be proud."

"Then why am I not proud of what I've accomplished? All I can think of is that I didn't even know that my best friend had passed away. That it would take a persistent woman to make me think of who I am and who I want to be. I'm not too sure I like the person I was, but I'm going to make sure I like the person I want to be."

There was a loud bark, and they saw that Nugget was coming in their direction. A smile of contentment covered his face as if he'd found some strange treasure. He flopped down on the ground and was soon fast asleep.

"The sun will soon be beating down. We should head back to the house."

"What do you want to do for the rest of the day?" she asked.

He grinned at her, his eyes aflame.

"While I do have a suggestion, it's really not advisable at this time. The doctor did say I shouldn't exert myself. I did disobey him last night."

"That's true. So you want to watch a movie or something? I have a large collection."

"That's fine. But we have to do your session first and then we can decide how to spend the day."

He groaned. "I thought you weren't feeling a hundred percent."

"I'm not, but you're doing fine. I'll put you through the paces. You just follow my instructions." He heard the hint of humor.

He chuckled, amusement flicking in his eyes. "I was hoping you'd want a break."

"Not taking any time off is how I'm going to be able to have you walking and using that hand in no time," she snapped. Her expression stilled and grew serious.

He remained silent.

"I'm sorry," she said softly. "I shouldn't have snapped. I know you're serious about your therapy. You've been working really hard. I'll go up and change and meet you in the gym in about thirty minutes."

She turned and walked away, leaving him standing alone.

He'd had every intention of working out. He'd made progress in the past week. He knew his hand and leg were getting better.

He walked in the direction she'd gone. He quickly changed into his gym gear and glanced at the clock.

He'd hang around for a bit and then go back downstairs.

He walked over to the dresser, glancing at a photo of his mother he'd kept all these years. It was strange, how when you kept items in plain view you didn't always see them. His mother had been a beautiful woman. He knew he'd taken most of his looks from her. He did carry some of his father's genes. He owed his physique to his father, but his face was definitely his mother's.

With the exception of the eyes. His eyes, a pale brown, almost amber in color, were one of the reasons he'd been so intriguing to modeling agencies. His well-toned body and handsome face had been appealing, but it had been his unusual eyes that had had agencies fighting for him. However, he'd remained with his first agency. They'd always been good to him, going beyond the call of duty to give him everything. He knew he'd made them money, but Chandra had become his friend.

She'd even insisted she could still use him after the accident, and she'd been right. He was sure that companies would have been content with face shots for their ads, but the idea of letting people see him in his broken state had forced him to turn down the offer. He couldn't let people in the industry see him as he was. He could imagine the looks of sympathy he'd get. He'd had enough of people's pity when he'd been in hospital during those awful months. He'd made the right decision for him. Being home was the best place for healing, especially now that Aaliyah had forced him into fighting for his healing.

There was a knock on his door.

"Dominic, is something wrong? I've been waiting for you."

He glanced at the clock, surprised to see that almost an hour had passed. Had he been daydreaming that long?

"Coming!" he shouted.

He quickly slipped into his sneakers and headed to the door. He opened it, immediately noticing her distance. He still wasn't sure what he'd done, but he was sure that in time he'd find out.

He followed her down the corridor, watching the sweet sway of her hips, despite her attempt to walk with stiff dignity.

"You could slow down," he said.

She stopped. "I don't have all morning, you know."

"Don't matter," he retorted. "Your mornings are all mine."

She gasped. "That's true, Mr. Wolfe. I keep forgetting you're the boss."

She turned and resumed walking, this time slowing her pace to something that was more manageable for him—a bit too manageable.

He followed along the corridor, which seemed longer than usual, and into the gym.

He sighed.

It was going to be a long morning.

Chapter 13

He breathed deeply and put the last weight down. His hand was sore, but he'd been able to lift the tiny weight with a lot more ease than when he'd started. In fact, Aaliyah had informed him that she would increase the weight for his next session. He squeezed his hand open and shut, feeling a sense of relief when he could do it with the minimum of pain. Tears welled in his eyes, but he fought them back. He would not cry. It was a sign of weakness he could not afford. He had to keep fighting. He had to be strong.

There was a knock at the door and Desmond entered.

"There's a young boy asking for you."

"A young boy?" he asked, but then Adrian's son came to mind. "Brandon."

"Yes, that's his name. I asked him to wait in the sitting room."

"Thanks. Tell him I'll be there shortly."

When Desmond was gone, he headed to his room. He didn't want to keep the Brandon waiting, but he needed to take a shower.

Twenty minutes later, he stepped into the sitting room to find Brandon chatting with Aaliyah.

Her soft laughter rippled through the air. Brandon giggled in return. Yesterday he'd seemed so serious and mature. Today he was a boy.

At the sound of his cane, they both looked in his direction.

Brandon stood, his discomfort evident. Dominic walked toward them, with what he hoped was a welcoming smile. He did not want to scare the boy away.

Aaliyah stood. "I'm going to leave you two gentlemen to chat." She turned to Brandon. "We're going to have to continue this conversation some other time. It was nice chatting with you."

"Nice to see you, too, Aaliyah."

As she passed him, she nodded nonchalantly. He wondered what was going through her mind.

With that, he turned to Brandon, glad to see him, but really not too sure what to say. He'd not had many interactions with teenagers. To him, they were a strange bunch, with the tight sagging pants showing their boxers. He was glad to see that Brandon was nicely dressed with a loose-fitting pair of jeans. He wasn't quite sure why it made him feel good, but it did.

Brandon moved toward him. He hesitated before he said, "I know you told me I could drop by anytime, but I wasn't sure. I hope dropping by today is fine."

Immediately, he saw the look in the boy's eyes. The boy was lonely, aching for a male role model in his life. He could see it in his hesitation. What he said right now could make a total difference in this boy's life.

"I did tell you coming over would be fine, and I meant it."

The boy's body relaxed noticeably. He'd said the right thing. Brandon no longer looked like a deer caught in the headlights of a car.

"I know I should have called first, but I was scared you'd say no."

"Why would I say no?"

"Look at your home. You have a beautiful home and beautiful girlfriend. You don't want for anything."

He heard a bit of himself in the boy's words.

"Money and fame isn't everything," he emphasized. "And Aaliyah's not my girlfriend. She's my therapist."

"Oh," he responded, but his eyes bore his skepticism.

"Yes, you see, I'm not too good without this cane right now. And my hand doesn't work too well, but they're getting better."

"What happened to your hand?"

"Maybe we could sit before I get into the details."

"Sorry," he said, concern in his voice. "Does it hurt to stand?"

"A bit, but it's not as bad as it was a few weeks ago. Aaliyah has worked miracles."

"She's good at what she does?"

"Yes, she's very good. She's my third therapist. I didn't get along well with the others."

"Are you are trying to say that you were difficult?" Brandon reasoned.

Dominic stared at Brandon. He noticed the wisdom in the boy's eyes, wisdom way beyond his age.

He nodded. "At that time, I was angry with the world."

"Are you still?"

"A bit, but I'm getting there. I've been trying real hard to look at life differently."

They'd reached the patio. Brandon waited until Dominic sat before him and then took the opposite couch.

"It's soon lunchtime. Want to stay for lunch?"

"If it's fine with you. I don't want to impose."

"As long as we call your grandmother and she says it's fine. Does she know you're here?"

"I told her that you were living here. She remembers you and says that you must come to see her."

Dominic remembered Mama, the old lady who'd often made sure he didn't go to bed hungry. For the second time in two days, he felt guilty. He'd avoided going to the village. Maybe it was about time he faced his demons.

"Tell her I'm going to come over as soon as I can. I can't drive and not sure I can walk that far right now, but I want to see her. She was good to me."

"Yeah, she's been good to me, as well. Just getting old in age. I do most of everything now. She has cancer."

"I'm so sorry to hear that."

"We're doing fine. Don't like to cook much, but I help her."

"You help with the cooking?" Dominic asked.

"Some of it. Mama can still get around, but I do as much as I can."

"And school?"

"I'm in high school. The same school my dad went to."

"My old school, too."

"That's cool. I should have guessed," Brandon said.

"Yeah, and you're doing well?"

"I'm a straight-A student. Grammy wouldn't accept anything else."

"Your dad would be proud," Dominic stated.

"I wish he was here. He always told me that my schoolwork was important. My dad made me promise that I'd make schoolwork priority. Fortunately, most of the other boys in the village are into their schoolwork, so it has been cool. We usually get together in the evenings to do our homework."

"That's so cool. Your dad and I were the only ones who were interested in any studying. We got teased a lot because of it. How old are you?"

"I'll be fourteen in August."

"That means you were born just after I left here."

At the same time, Mrs. Clarke entered the patio.

"Lunch is ready." She glanced in Brandon's direction, curiosity in her eyes. "I see we have a guest?"

Brandon rose to his feet immediately.

"This is Brandon. His father was my best friend when I lived here as a child."

"You're Adrian Johnson's son?"

"Yes, madam."

"You're just as handsome as your father. He was a heartbreaker. All the girls loved him. Sorry he passed away so young."

"Thanks, madam. I still miss him."

"You can call me Mrs. Clarke. I ain't nobody's madam."

Brandon smiled and nodded.

"Well, come," Mrs. Clarke continued. "Aaliyah is waiting on the two of you. I'm sure she's hungry by now."

Dominic rose from the chair, reaching for his cane.

"Hope you like spaghetti and meatballs, young man," Mrs. Clarke said with a twinkle in her eyes.

"I love spaghetti and meatballs." Brandon beamed.

"Good, 'cause I make the best on the island. Even better than those fancy restaurants."

"And I am living proof that she's better," Dominic added. "She's the best cook on the island."

"I'm sure my grandmother will have something to say about that."

"Mama? I haven't seen her in ages. She taught me to cook so many years ago. How is she doing?"

"She's not doing too well," Brandon replied, "but

she has her Bible and her faith. They give her comfort."

"Yes, she does. I suspected something was wrong with her. I don't get into the village too often. On my days off I head to St. Michael to see my daughter and her kids. I'm going to make a promise to come visit her when I'm off next week."

"I'm sure she will be glad to see you."

They'd reached the dining room, where Aaliyah sat patiently waiting for them. The slight frown on her face morphed into a broad smile when she saw them.

"Told you she was hungry," Mrs. Clarke said. "Enjoy your meal."

When she disappeared, a barely recognizable rendition of Rihanna's "We Found Love" followed her. They all laughed.

"She's Rihanna's number-one fan on the island," Dominic offered.

"I would have thought Rihanna's music would be a bit risqué for her," Aaliyah said.

"Oh, those are the ones she likes more. Wait until you hear and see her rendition of 'S&M.' It's hilarious."

"I can imagine, but instead of talking about Mrs. Clarke and Rihanna at this moment, can we eat?" Aaliyah asked.

At the same time, Brandon's stomach grumbled. They laughed.

Brandon, trying not to look too embarrassed, said, "I'm sorry. I didn't realize I was so hungry."

"Let's dig in."

* * *

Lunch was a mixture of laugher and discussion about anything under the sun. Aaliyah was amazed at the knowledge Brandon possessed. She was glad to hear he was doing well in school, and like her, loved to read. He wanted to be a lawyer and was hoping he would be awarded a scholarship.

One of the things the three of them had in common was their love of movies. Again she was surprised when Brandon's taste not only included the latest action movies, but movies with critical acclaim, which she was sure the average teenage boy wouldn't touch with a ten-foot pole.

After lunch, they decided to watch the Academy Award-winning *Life of Pi.*

Two hours later, after the credits had rolled, they'd had an interesting discussion regarding the merits and weaknesses of the movie. Brandon announced that he had to leave.

"So soon," she said, realizing that Dominic, too, looked disappointed. He was great company.

"I have to go take care of my grandmother and make sure she eats. She cooks and then refuses to eat. Of course, she likes me to sit and talk with her when she's watching *her soap operas.*"

From the expression on his face, she could tell he wasn't too happy about the arrangement.

"It's not my kind of show," he confirmed, "but I know she gets lonely, so if having to endure a show for an hour or so each day makes her happy, then I'm going to do it."

"That's really cool of you," Dominic said.

"I love Grammy, and if spending some time with her is all she asks, then I'll do it. It makes her happy."

"So what are your plans for the rest of the week?"

"The boys and I are going into the city tomorrow and the next day we're going to the cinema."

"So you have a pretty packed few days?"

"Yes," he replied, nodding. He hesitated. "Would it be okay if I come by on Saturday sometime?"

"As long as you don't have a problem with hanging with us old folks."

"Speak for yourself. I assure you I'm not old," Aaliyah said.

"Neither of you are old. I'm sure you can't be over thirty."

"Thanks, Brandon. You're the kind of gentleman I like. I'm sure one day you'll be breaking hearts."

"I've been told I'm already breaking hearts and I'm not even trying. I'm focusing on my studies and that's the only thing that's important."

"I'm glad to hear you say that."

"So I'll see you on Saturday? I have soccer practice in the morning, so it won't be until around midday."

"That's cool. You can come for lunch."

"Okay, but I don't want Mrs. Clarke to think I'm only coming over to eat."

"It's cool, Brandon. I know that's not why you're coming over."

"Cool. 'Bye, I really need to get home now."

"I'll see you on Saturday."

He turned and walked away, but not before she saw

the glimmer of sadness in his eyes. Aaliyah could tell he loved being over there, loved being around Dominic.

"I'm scared for him," Dominic said. "I can see he misses his father. I hope he doesn't start seeing me as a replacement for his father."

She grunted. "And what's wrong with that?"

"The boy needs a man in his life. I'm not that man."

"But I can tell you like having him over. Why invite him over, then? You're going to break that boy's heart," she stated.

"Can't I just be friends with the boy without people starting to think we're a match made in heaven?"

"I think you'd make a great dad," she said. "The boy has no one. He'll soon not have his grandmother. Who's going to take care of him?"

"Aaliyah, can you hear yourself? I just met the boy yesterday and already you have me adopting him."

She looked at him, tears glistening in her eyes.

"I'm sorry. I just feel so sorry for him. He has no one. He could be out there doing drugs and getting ready to break into someone's house. Instead, he spent the afternoon with us discussing a movie that most boys his age would consider boring. What else do you want me to think?"

"What do you want me to do?" he shouted.

"All I know is that that young boy needs someone and he doesn't have a clue what's going on in his life. He's reaching out to you."

"I'll have to think about this," he snapped. "I'm going to my workshop."

"Running away is not going to stop you from feeling what you feel."

"And what am I feeling?"

"You already love that boy. In him you see your best friend. And you're scared, because you know if you let that boy in, you won't be able to look at his life and do nothing."

"Along with being a therapist, you're a psychologist, too," he said, shrugging his shoulders.

"Of course not, I just know you."

He picked up his cane, nodded at her and walked away.

When he was gone, she poured a glass of wine and walked out onto the patio. She took a sip, though she wanted to gulp the whole bottle down.

Life was so strange. She couldn't believe that so much had happened to her in such a short space of time. It had barely been a month and already she'd immersed herself into the household.

She couldn't imagine leaving the island when she was done. She didn't expect anything else from Dominic. While she was here, she expected that they'd continue to make love. However, she didn't expect more. She could see already that Dominic had a problem with commitment.

Even now, the anger still boiled inside her. She could see things so clearly and he couldn't. It frustrated her that he couldn't see Brandon's need. But she knew she was being unreasonable. Dominic was trying to deal with his own issues and she was forcing something else on him. She was being idealistic. She didn't even know if Dominic could take care of himself. While he'd been making great progress, it would take months, years even, for him to regain full use of his hand and leg. While she could tell his hand was healing well and responding to the therapy, his leg was another matter. But she knew miracles did happen. While she'd only been a therapist for a short time, as a nurse, she'd seen amazing things that made her even more convinced that miracles still happened.

While Dominic and his relationships were worrisome, her own relationship with him scared her. At present she had no expectations, but each day she wanted more.

Did he have more to offer? He was affectionate, but she knew that he would always see his injury as a burden to whomever he was involved with.

She was the other problem. What was she going to do with her life? She'd not thought of what would happen after she left the island.

The obvious would be to return to the hospital, but she wasn't sure if that was what she wanted. She wasn't sure if remaining on the island was an option. But she couldn't leave the island knowing how she felt about Dominic.

She was slowly but surely falling in love with him. She didn't want it to happen and didn't think it was a sensible thing to do. But one thing she realized was that she didn't have control over her feelings.

That was love. It crept up on you and slammed you in the face.

What she felt for Dominic was so different from Andrew. Her marriage had been comfortable. With Dominic, things were different. His lovemaking was different. Even though his leg and hand weren't functioning well, his lovemaking was off the charts. She'd been pleasantly surprised when she'd realized that his leg injury hadn't affected him in bed much.

The ringing of her cell phone drew her from her musings. She glanced down. It was Eboni.

"What's wrong?" she said as soon as she connected the call. "It is time?"

Eboni laughed. "No, Aaliyah. You know I have another month to go before the babies are born. I can't believe you've been there all that time and you haven't given me a call, except when you first arrived. Is the job keeping you that busy?"

She wondered what would be the best way to calm her sister. Time was moving so fast. She couldn't believe she had not thought about calling.

"It has been so hectic here. I was planning to call you over the weekend."

"But you didn't even have to call. Remember social media? There are so many ways we could've kept in contact."

"I'm sorry, Eboni. There is no excuse for not calling. How are the babies?"

"They were doing fine my last checkup. They are doing much better than Darren is. He's a wreck. Worrying about everything. He went to his first Lamaze class with me and almost fainted. But he's a trooper, he came back and endured it. He has even bonded with some of the other fathers-to-be, so they seem to be commiserating with each other."

"I'm glad to know you are both doing fine. Please make sure he calls me when you go into labor."

"I'm going to call. I know he's not going to be in any state to make phone calls until these babies are out." She laughed.

"So how are you doing? Who's this mysterious boss of yours?"

Aaliyah breathed in deeply. She didn't want to gush or sound overenthusiastic. While she would eventually share her relationship with Eboni, she didn't want to be presumptuous about their current status.

"I'm doing fine. The work is nothing that I can't manage. In fact, I only do my sessions with him in the morning and that's it until the next day."

"So who is *he?*"

"Are you sure you're ready for this?"

"This has to be a big one…"

"Dominic Wolfe."

"Dominic Wolfe? Are you kidding me?" Eboni screamed.

"No, I'm not."

"Girl, let me sit down so I can hear all the juicy details. The man is the bomb. I'd get on a plane right now to let him scratch my tummy."

Aaliyah giggled.

"Is he as gorgeous in person as he is on television

and in magazines? Lord, he's the only man that could give Darren some competition."

"Eboni, stop kidding. You know you're totally devoted to Darren."

"Yes, but I can fantasize, can't I? Darren fantasizes about Kerry Washington all the time. I told him the other night that if he doesn't stop watching *Scandal* with his eyes glued to her, I'm going to divorce him. You know what he told me in response? If I did he'd probably go marry her. The nerve of that man."

They both laughed.

"But I'm still waiting. Is he just as gorgeous?"

"Yes, and more. He's one of the sexiest men I've ever met, but he's hurting and troubled."

"He is?"

"Yes, when I first met him, I'm not sure I was impressed at all. Did you know he was hurt in a fire?"

"I think I'd heard about it. Didn't he save some girl's life and become a big hero?"

"Yes, he did. But it doesn't appear many knew that he was hurt trying to save the girl. The building fell in on them and he was pinned under debris before someone came to his rescue. It pinned his left side, so his left hand and leg were damaged. He couldn't walk for weeks, but he's recovering now."

"Your hands have the magic touch...even when you were just nursing. I'm glad to hear you're enjoying your job. Maybe you can really help him. I'm sure he must be all down and depressed."

"Not really. More angry with the world and about

the blow that fate dealt him. But I guess I would be, too, under the circumstances."

"Anger may be his motivation for working at healing. Now, I need to give you some news. The private investigator, Carlos, just called. Seems like he has a good lead on Cindi and Keisha's whereabouts."

Aaliyah sat up immediately, unable to say anything. Tears welled in her eyes.

"Aaliyah, are you all right?"

"I'll be fine. I'm just so happy. I couldn't have heard better news."

"He promised to call back as soon as he talks to them."

"Please tell them to call me as soon as you talk to them."

"You know you don't have to ask that. We've been waiting for this so long. I wanted to get on a plane and go with Carlos. Of course, Darren would hear nothing of it."

"Are you crazy? Of course you can't get on a plane. You're too far along."

"It was worth a try."

"You have to trust Carlos. He's done good work. Didn't he find me?"

"That's true. Oh, Aaliyah, I can't contain myself. I hope I can convince them to get on a plane and come see me. They may have to wait a bit to see you."

Sadness washed over her. "I didn't think of that."

"You'll be fine. Your time in Barbados will be up in no time and you'll be back home celebrating with all of your sisters."

"Eboni, that sounds so good. I can't wait to see them. I wonder what they're doing. If they've married, had kids or are still studying…"

"We'll get all of those answers in time. Well, my husband is calling me, so I'll have to go. He says hi and tells you to find a sexy Barbadian and get married."

"That's not what I'm here for."

"Maybe you can jump Dominic's bones. That would be worth all the effort."

She did not reply to her sister's comment. If Eboni only knew that she'd already jumped his bones, and more.

"Okay, this conversation needs to end right now. He's my boss and that's it."

"If you say so. He's your boss, but that doesn't stop him from oozing sexy. If I were you, I'd make sure you get some. I'm sure he'd be worth every minute. And before you respond, I'll say goodbye. Love you. I will call as soon as I hear from Carlos. Good night, sister of mine."

With that, she disconnected the call, leaving Aaliyah feeling frustrated and bothered.

She didn't like lying to her sister.

Chapter 14

Dominic placed the finished sculpture on the table on display and went to the sink to wash his hands. He looked at the piece and was pleased with what he saw. He glanced at the clock. It was just after three o'clock in the morning. He hadn't been able to go back to sleep, so he'd decided to try his hand at another project. It had not been difficult to visualize Nugget, and the finished piece captured the energy he'd wanted it to. The fingers of his left hand hurt a bit, but Aaliyah had promised that the exercise would cause no harm, if he took it easy.

He headed to his room. When he opened the door, he stopped abruptly. Aaliyah was lying in his bed, fast asleep. He noticed the tearstains on her cheek. She'd been crying. He ached to comfort her, but decided he really needed to take a bath before he did.

When he came out the bathroom, she was still fast asleep. About to head to his dresser to find a pair of shorts, he changed his mind and crawled into the bed. He noticed that she, too, was naked under the covers and marveled at her lack of inhibition. After they'd made love and showered, she'd asked him for a shirt, but he'd pulled her into the bed naked and she'd blushed, her innocence refreshing. He still could not believe she'd been married. Her air of innocence still fascinated him.

When he drew closer to her, she stirred, her eyes opening slowly.

"Sorry, I didn't mean to wake you."

She stared at him, confusion on her face, and then she smiled.

"I'm glad to see you smile. You were crying?" He raised his hand to press a finger where the tearstains remained.

"My sister Eboni called. The private investigator has found our sisters."

He struggled to contain his excitement. He was happy for her.

"You've spoken to them already? Where did she find them?"

"I haven't spoken to them yet. When Eboni called, the investigator had just left New York to find them."

"You're sure he's not pulling a con on your sister to get more money?"

She looked at him in shock. "Carlos? Definitely not. Carlos is the epitome of honesty."

"As long as you're sure."

"I'm sure," she replied. "Carlos came highly recommended. I've had no problems with him."

"So your tears are of joy?"

"Yes."

"I know." He could hear the tiredness in her voice. "Let's go to sleep. I know you're tired. I didn't mean to wake you."

"It's fine. I'm not sleepy anymore." Her voice was soft and husky.

"You aren't?"

"No, I'm not."

"So what do you want to do?"

"I'm not sure. Maybe read a book."

"I can think of something a lot more fun than reading."

"You can? But reading is lots of fun for me."

He eased closer to her, pressing his body against her side.

"Something's poking me in the side," she said. "Let's see what it is." He felt her fingers trace along her leg until she gripped his erection in her hand.

She shifted on the bed, urging him to lie on his back. He complied, his excitement intensifying with the anticipation.

She raised herself over him, lowering herself onto his body, careful not to hurt his arm or side.

She slid her body upward and downward until his penis strained against her, hoping for release.

Her lips covered his boldly. She moved from his lips and slowly worked herself downward.

When she reached his chest, she placed her hands on his nipples, kneading them between her fingers. Heat surged through him as her tongue explored his nipples. She squeezed one and he shuddered with the pleasure.

Her mouth explored every inch of his body as she moved downward. His penis jerked in anticipation, but when her lips covered the hardness of his erection, he heard his cry of pleasure fill the room.

As he lay there, she worked her magic, taking him to the point of release only to pull him back again. His body bucked and shuddered. And when he could bear it no more and felt the pressure build inside, he screamed.

When they were done, he reached for her. "Take a shower with me."

She followed him.

In the shower, they kissed, water cascading around them, and then the unexpected happened.

His body hardened again, and he turned her to face the wall, bending her slightly to maximize his entry. When his penis slipped inside the moistness of her vagina, her cry of pleasure filled the room. He stroked her hard and fast.

Soon his body tensed and as he felt the hot surge along the length of his manhood, he slowed to a circular grind, letting her feel every inch of his thick, turgid length. When his release came, he bellowed her name, resting against her back, as she cried out with the intensity of her own release.

When his head hit the pillow after they'd showered, he fell instantly asleep.

When Aaliyah woke next morning, the bed was empty. Between the curtains of the patio door, she could see the first glimmer of light. She rose from the bed, placing a robe around her before she walked over to the door and slipped between the curtains.

Dominic stood, leaning against the railing, looking down the sloped area that led to the gardens and the ocean in the distance.

He was naked, and she felt the familiar stir of desire. She could not get enough of him and wondered how she could ever leave and return home.

He turned at the sound of her feet and smiled, a smile that didn't quite reach his eyes. Something worried him, and she hastened toward him.

"What's wrong?" she asked.

When she reached him, she pressed her body against him. Slowly his arms came up and held her.

"Don't hurt your hand," she said.

"I won't. I know I must be careful, but I have to try to use it as much as possible."

"You're okay?" she asked.

"Yes, just thinking. A lot of things have been happening."

She nodded, encouraging him to speak.

"I was thinking about Brandon. What's going to happen to him? He only has his grandmother."

"I'm sure his grandmother must be worried about him and what will happen once she is gone. She did tell you to come see her."

"I don't even know how to take care of a child. I haven't particularly liked them in the past."

"But he really isn't a boy anymore. In no time he'll be sixteen."

"What if I want to get married? What woman would want a ready-made son?"

"A woman who loves you. I just think you're finding excuses where there really are none. My suggestion is to talk to his grandmother first."

He nodded. "I'll try to see her as soon as I can."

"No, let's go tomorrow. I can drive you into the village."

She could see his hesitation.

"Okay, I'll go. Just so I can put my mind at rest."

"You said there was something else."

"Yeah, but can we talk about it later today."

"No problem."

He reached for her and gently guided her to stand in front of him. He placed both hands around her until her body curved into this.

"This is the time of the day I love most on the island."

She gazed ahead of her. The sun, asleep for most of the night, had peeped its head out.

Aaliyah knew the sunrise could be a wonderful display of nature's colors, and this morning did not disappoint. They watched as the final shades of gray disappeared to be replaced by dull shades of blue, until the shades of the sun mixed with the blue. Dominic pointed to the left and there, nestled among the trees, a rainbow arched, and its kaleidoscope of colors was as vivid and alive as the skies.

"It's so beautiful," Aaliyah screamed in joy. "I've never seen anything so beautiful."

"I have."

"What do you mean?"

"You. You are beautiful."

She giggled, feeling her body warm with pleasure again.

"I am?" she said coyly.

"Yes, you are beautiful. Outside." He placed a finger under her chin, tilting her face so she looked up at him. The other hand he pressed against her head. "And inside."

She placed her hands around him, hugging him tightly. She wanted to say so much to him, but she didn't. She wasn't sure what she wanted to say, and neither did she think he was ready to hear it. She knew that his feelings were one of the things on his mind, as they were on hers.

He lowered his head to kiss her, but she placed a finger to his lips.

"I would suggest we go inside if I'm right about where this is going. You are naked, you know."

"I'd love to make love to you out here someday, but I'm sure that Mrs. Clarke wouldn't approve. You might be surprised, but Mrs. Clarke has a gentleman friend who drops by on occasion. She doesn't even know I know he sleeps over from time to time."

He laughed at the incredulous look on her face. "Now come let me take you inside and show you how much I love to make love to you."

"You do? You've never told me."

"No need to tell you. I assure you, I'm much better at showing."

She turned to move into the bedroom and he followed her inside.

He wanted to make love to her so badly. It had taken all of his power to control himself.

Chapter 15

Later, when Aaliyah awoke, the humming of rain greeted her. She could not believe that the early promise of sunshine had dissipated. She walked to the bathroom, took a quick shower and went in search of Dominic. She headed to his workshop first, knowing that he would either be there or in the gym.

She chided herself. She'd missed their usual morning session. Why hadn't Dominic awoken her?

When she reached his workshop, she pushed the door open gently, not wanting to disturb his creative process.

He sat among the shadows, the only light a single bulb over his head. He was engrossed in his project, and from where he stood she could tell he was using both hands, but she hoped he didn't overdo it. While she was concerned, she could not help but admire his determination.

She realized he'd not noticed her and started to step forward when she halted. The floor creaked and he turned immediately, shifting his body to hide what he was working on.

"Did you have breakfast?" he asked.

She took another step forward and he raised his hand up.

"I'm really sorry, but I'm working on something very special. I promise you'll be the first one to see it."

She stepped backward as if she'd been slapped in the face. She hesitated. His comment had hurt her, though she knew he was working on something special.

"Don't be hurt. I promise you, you're going to love it when you see it."

She smiled, wanting to reassure him, but knew the smile didn't quite reach her eyes. Why was she being so silly?

"I'll go downstairs and have breakfast. I'm a bit hungry."

He placed a white sheet of plastic over the sculpture and rose, walking as fast as he could toward her.

"I should be done later this evening. I'll come for you then. Please tell Mrs. Clarke she can bring my lunch here."

He bent his head to touch her lips with his. The kiss was slow and searching. Hers yielded and her body shivered in response.

When his lips left her she felt empty. She ached.
"I promise I'll come to you later."

She smiled, realizing he needed her reassurance.

She reached a hand up and caressed his cheek.
"We're fine," she said. She tilted her head upward
and kissed him on the cheek.

She smiled again, turned and walked through the
door. The only sound she heard was the soft click of
the door as it closed.

Dominic walked toward the worktable. He stared
at the project he'd started a few nights ago. Every
night after Aaliyah fell asleep, he would come to the
studio for about an hour and work on it. He was working in clay. While he could work with several other
materials, clay was his favorite. His preference was
something he couldn't explain. Under his hands a
piece of clay came alive until he could feel its warmth
and power.

It was like his acting. When he took on a new
role, he became that character, as if the character was
alive inside him and the breath he took was theirs
and not his.

He knew that he needed to take a break. His hand
was feeling sore and tired, but he didn't want to stop.
He'd promised Aaliyah she could see it this evening,
so he had to be finished.

He also had to give Brandon a call, find out if he
was still coming over on the weekend.

He also needed to go see Mama.

He picked up his cell phone and dialed the number.

"Hello."

"Brandon, it's Dominic. How are you doing?"

"I'm fine. Just here doing some studying. I have an assignment to submit on Friday. Just wanted to have it done early."

"That's good. Sorry to disturb you."

"It's fine. I was planning to give you a call, but…"

"Brandon, let's just make this clear now. You can call me anytime, and as long as your grandmother says it's fine you can come over."

"Okay. I'm just worried you're doing this because you're my dad's friend and feel sorry for me."

"I'll be honest. You are my best friend's son. But I like you. You're a decent young man. You need someone. I want to help, if it's all right with you."

"I'm fine with it. Just make sure you let me know when I'm being a nuisance. I like hanging with my friends, but I enjoyed hanging with you and your girl."

"My therapist!" Dominic emphasized.

"Oops, I forgot, *your therapist*."

Dominic could hear the amusement in the boy's voice.

"Good, let me talk to your grandmother now. I hope she remembers me."

"Oh, she does. She's your biggest fan. She's watched all of your movies. Don't tell her I told you this, but she has a scrapbook of photos and newspaper and magazine clippings. She also has the DVDs of all your movies."

"I won't tell," he promised.

"Okay." The phone went silent for a moment and he heard Brandon shouting for his grandmother in the distance.

He heard the phone shuffling, and then Mama's voice.

"Hello."

"Hi, Mrs. Johnson."

"Who you think you calling Mrs. Johnson? I was Mama when you were a little boy and I'm still Mama."

He laughed. A warm feeling bubbled inside. Mama was the same old vibrant outspoken Mama.

"So when you planning on come see me? I can't believe you live in that old plantation house and haven't come and visited me yet. But I forgive ya. Brandon says you got hurt in a fire trying to help a little girl. I always knew you were the one who had heart. I'm really proud of you." He loved her use of the Bajan dialect. It made him feel warm and at home.

"Thanks, Mama."

"You ain't got to thank me. You work hard to achieve all you have. Not like some of these lazy-ass boys who went to school with you and still ain't work a day."

"I've been trying," he responded.

"So when you coming to see me?"

"I'll get my driver, Desmond, to drive me over tomorrow."

"Desmond!" she screeched. "You mean that sweet talking playboy? He ain't know what he want out of life. 'Bout time he settled down. Still running behind all the skirts. You won't remember him, but he was a young boy when you left the island. But he's a good boy. He hardworking."

"I didn't even know he was from the village. Who's his mother?"

"Don't you remember Margo? She's the woman with quite a few children, but she always made sure she took care of them. I'm sure she had a son close to your age. What's his name now?" There was a pause. "Yes, his name is William. He was tall and handsome just like Desmond."

An image of a boy he played with flashed in his mind. No wonder Desmond had always looked familiar.

"Well, this boy here wants to talk to you again. Looks like he wants to take the phone from me."

"I'll see you when I pass by tomorrow."

"Yes, I'm looking forward to seeing you, too. Want to see if you as handsome as those photos."

With a final good-night, she was gone.

"Thanks for chatting with her. It made her day," Brandon said.

"It was great to talk to her. She was always kind to me. I wanted to ask you what you were doing over the weekend."

"I have a football match on Saturday morning and nothing else for the rest of the weekend. I go to church with Mama on Sundays."

"I'll talk to her when I drop by tomorrow afternoon. How would you like to spend the weekend here?"

"You're serious?"

"If you grandmother agrees."

"I'm sure she will. She lets me go spend the week-end at my friends'. But I don't want to intrude."

"What did I say to you? You want to come and spend the weekend?"

"Yeah, I'd like that."

"Good."

"You sure your gi—therapist won't mind?"

"I'm sure she won't. She likes you."

"She does? She is pretty."

"She thinks you're a fine young man," Dominic emphasized.

"She does?"

"Yes, she does. Good, I'll talk to you tomorrow. You have a good night, son."

There was silence and he realized what he'd said.

"Good night. I'll see you tomorrow."

The phone disconnected and he stood staring at it before he finally put it down. The boy was already working himself into his heart.

Aaliyah watched Dominic from the corner of her eyes. He was reading, but she could tell his thoughts were elsewhere.

"A penny for them," she said, drawing closer to where he lay on the bed.

He looked up, perplexed by what she'd said. And then it dawned on him.

"Just thinking about things?" she asked.

"About Brandon," he replied.

"What about him?"

"I asked him if he wanted to spend the weekend here."

She could not hide her joy.

"I knew you wouldn't have a problem with it."

"I'm going over to see his grandmother tomorrow. Want to come with me?"

"Are you sure?"

"She told me to make sure I brought *my girl-friend.*"

She laughed.

"And of course, you emphasized that I am your therapist?"

"Yes, I was sure to. Of course, Brandon doesn't believe a word I said about you."

"Unless he sees something definite, he can only assume. I am going to sleep in my room when he is here."

"I'm going to put him in a room at the other side of the house."

"You will do no such thing. I'm sure you can live a few days with…"

"I'm going to come to your room during the night, and no one's going to stop me."

"Don't I have a say in this since it's my room we're talking about?"

"If you say so, but remember I have all the keys to the kingdom."

She smiled. "That is true, but there is one thing you can't lock or unlock."

"And I'd like to know what that is," he teased.

"I'm sure you know exactly what I mean."

"If you do mean what I'm thinking about, I can unlock it with a simple touch." He pressed the palm of his hand against that special place between her legs. Flames ignited, making her feel hot and tingly.

"I admire a man who's confident. However, we were talking about going to do your workout."

"We can't work out this evening. I want to show you what I've been working on."

"Oh, you did promise me."

"So you're ready to see the masterpiece?"

"I definitely am. Lead the way."

He picked up his cane and walked toward the door. He stopped and turned to her. "You have to promise me you won't laugh. It's far from perfect, but I think it's the most beautiful thing I've ever created."

She continued toward his workshop while he followed her. He was walking much better, but she was sure he did not realize.

When they reached the studio, she opened the door and he followed her in.

"You stay here. Let me make sure all is ready."

She paused and watched as he walked toward the workbench. "You can come over now," he said, several minutes later.

When she reached the workbench, she could not believe what she saw.

He'd done a sculpture of her. She was almost naked, but he'd draped her in a cloth. Only her shoulders and the curve and rise of her breasts were exposed.

But that was not what he had focused on. It was her face and the air of innocence and vulnerability that the image possessed.

She wanted to say something, but she wasn't even sure what she wanted to say. She didn't know that tears had started to trickle down her cheeks until she felt the dampness.

Finally, she said, "It's beautiful."

It was not perfect, she acknowledged, but it was truly beautiful. He'd somehow been able to capture the essence of who she was.

"I'm glad you like it."

"I love it! It must have taken you lots of time."

"It really didn't. I enjoyed working on it. I'm just sorry it's not perfect."

"I think the message it delivers is perfect. I've learned in the past few weeks that even at my age, I'm still growing and becoming the person I want to be."

"I've been thinking the same thing, thanks to you."

"I know you have," she said.

"Maybe all that has happened in my life is part of a bigger plan. I've been thinking about my modeling, my acting, my art. I know I now have to make decisions about my life and my future. Which is more important? What I want to do with the rest of my life? What I want to do for Brandon?"

"I'm sure you'll do what's right for you. I think I've finally resolved all I was feeling about my husband. I know he would want me to be happy. I've not been involved with anyone since his death and there was a part of me that felt guilty responding to someone else. I did feel that way with you at first."

"For me, it's understandable. You loved your husband. He loved you. You had a life together. I don't expect you to just stop loving him."

She stared at him for a while. His words offered some reassurance.

"But it doesn't mean I can't love again."

"I'm glad to know that. You'll make some lucky man a great wife."

At the same time, her cell phone rang, breaking the mood of expectation.

It was Eboni.

"Hello, Eboni," she said. Her heart was beating fast.

"Aaliyah, I just spoke to Cindi." Aaliyah could tell she'd been crying.

"What's wrong?"

"I'm just crying because I'm happy. I gave her your number, so she's going to call you sometime before the day is over. I haven't spoken to Keisha yet. She's in Europe backpacking, so Cindi is not sure when she's going to hear from her. Cindi says she's a bit of a free spirit. She made some bad choices but is trying to find herself," Eboni said.

"I'm so sorry I couldn't be there for her. I feel as if I've let them down," Aaliyah replied.

"They don't blame either of us. They were adopted by the same couple, but Keisha didn't seem to be able to deal with it. Cindi has done pretty well. She's a teacher."

"Oh, my God, she's a teacher! We've got to see how we can help them."

"Aaliyah, they are big girls. They have to make their own choices just like you and I did. We're not even sure if they really want to be part of our lives."

"How could they not?" Aaliyah argued. "We are their sisters."

"Yes, we are, by blood, but so many years have passed. You and I, we're just now growing accustomed to each other again. Remember, we were closer in age than they were. They were just little kids."

"That's true," Aaliyah replied, nodding her head. "I've always had this image in my mind that when we find each other, it will all be great. We'll get together, move in with each other and live happily ever after."

"Sounds perfect, doesn't it? But that's really not the reality that we face."

She did not reply. What Eboni was saying was true.

"You remember those fairy tales Mom read to us every night? I'd always imagined my life like one of those stories. But it's so far from that."

"You do realize that most of the girls in those stories didn't have it easy. But eventually they did find love. I've found it, but like in those stories, finding happiness and my happily ever after didn't come easy."

"I'm glad you are living your romance. I'm a lot more skeptical. I've lived with reality."

"So have I, but I still continued to believe that there is a hero out there for each of us."

Aaliyah shifted her eyes to where Dominic sat, engrossed in whatever he was doing. She noticed his hands, the fact that his weaker hand was working a lot faster.

"I think I know what you mean."

"You've met someone, Aaliyah."

"Yes, but we're going to have to talk about that at another time."

"He's there?"

"Yes."

"Dominic?"

"Yes."

"Oh, my God. You have to call me tomorrow when you can talk."

"Definitely."

"Have a good night."

"I will. Talk to you tomorrow."

"Of course."

"'Bye."

"'Bye."

"Take care of those babies."

"I will."

The phone disconnected.

"How is your sister doing?"

"She's fine. The babies are due in a few weeks."

"I'm glad to know."

"Are you ready for bed?" she asked.

"Yes, I'm tired. I need to get some sleep tonight."

"Well, that's what nights are for." She laughed.

"I'll be there in a bit. I just want to finish planning this new project."

"I'm going up to get ready for bed."

He turned back to his workbench and she walked away smiling. There would be no sleep tonight.

Chapter 16

The next morning, the sound of her cell phone's rendition of *Star Trek*'s theme song woke her. She reached for the phone, not recognizing the number, but answered, wondering if it were Cindi.

"Aaliyah, it's Cindi."

Tears immediately sprang into her eyes. She could not speak.

"Aaliyah?"

"I'm sorry," she stammered. "I've been waiting for this moment for so long, I'm not even sure what to say."

"Just say you're glad to hear from me."

"Of course I'm glad to hear from you."

Dominic stirred beside her, his eyes opening. She'd awakened him.

"Sorry," she whispered. "It's my sister."

He nodded in return. He closed his eyes and buried himself back into the covers.

"Eboni told me she spoke to you yesterday. I couldn't wait until this morning to call. I'm sorry I called so early, but I have to go into work. I wouldn't have gotten the chance to call until tonight."

"That's fine. It's time for me to get up anyway."

"So you're in Barbados. The island must be awesome. I've heard a lot of my friends talking about their holidays there. I hope I can take a trip there someday."

"Eboni told me you are a teacher?"

"Yes, I teach kindergarten."

"Nurturing small minds. It must be fascinating."

"It usually is, but it can also be challenging. You know kids. Sweet and adorable until they decide to throw a tantrum."

"I still think it's fascinating."

"Eboni told me you were a nurse and finished your physiotherapist qualification a few months ago."

"Yes, I've been studying part-time for quite a while now. Took me a bit longer to finish, but I didn't want to give up my job at the hospital, so part-time was the best alternative."

"And you're now in Barbados?"

"Yes, I'm a private nurse and therapist. I'm working for Dominic Wolfe."

"Oh, my God. Dominic Wolfe? You mean the model turned actor? He is simply dreamy. I love him in the small indie movie he did a couple of years ago.

Not like the blockbusters he does, but it was really good."

"I'm not sure I've seen that one. I thought he was only a big movie star."

"No, this movie went through the film-festival circuit and even won a prize at Cannes. He was to get a major role in an upcoming film and dropped out. No one has seen him since. I didn't realize he was in Barbados."

"Yes, he was born here. Just a short distance from where his home is."

"Sounds interesting. I'd love to come to Barbados, but I don't know when I'm eligible for holiday, since I just started."

"So what about Keisha?"

"What do I say about Keisha... Some people think she's crazy. But to me, she's brave and bold, creative and adventurous. She's backpacking across Europe with friends right now. She sends postcards from each place she visits, but we haven't talked since she left."

"What did she do before she left?"

"Oh, she's an investigative journalist. Something happened at work that she didn't quite like, so she left."

"Any knowledge as to when she'll be back?"

"I'm not sure and I don't think she's sure, either, but a rough estimate would be another two months. I know she's in Spain right now."

"I'm glad she's doing something that makes her happy."

"Well, Aaliyah, I have to go. Duty calls."

"'Bye. Thanks for calling. Love you."

"Love you, too."

Aaliyah placed the phone down. She could feel the tears in her eyes.

"Was that your sister?" Dominic asked.

"Yes, Cindi. She's a kindergarten teacher. I can't believe it. She sounds so mature."

She started to cry.

Dominic pulled her toward him, holding her as she cried tears of joy.

When the car pulled up at the house where he'd spent so much of his childhood days, he was surprised at all of the changes. The once simple chattel house had been converted into a modern structure. While it was still not elaborate, the old jalousie windows had been replaced by iron. The wooden structure itself had been replaced by walls.

Adrian had done a great job on his home. It saddened him that his friend had not lived to see him.

The front door opened and Brandon rushed outside, his face showing his excitement. One of the boys who'd been on the beach followed him, trying to contain his own enthusiasm.

Next to him, Aaliyah placed the car in Park.

"Not bad. You didn't have much of a problem driving on the left-hand side of the road," Dominic said.

"It felt a bit awkward at first, but since we didn't have to go too far, it wasn't a problem. I just felt a bit panicky when we passed that car on the main road."

When she unlocked her door, he did the same,

stepping out without his cane. While this may not have been the best time to see how he could walk without his cane, she'd agreed to his suggestion. He was still using the cane, but he could manage without it, though he had to move slower.

Before he could get out of the car, Brandon was standing next to him, a wide grin on his face.

"Hi, Dominic. This is my best friend, Kemar. He usually stays over on Saturdays after football practice. Of course, since he realized you are one of his favorite movie stars he's been excited to meet you again. He still can't believe he didn't recognize you when we were at the beach."

The shy teenager stepped forward. "A pleasure to meet you, sir. I love your movies."

"You can call me Dominic. I'm glad you enjoy my movies."

"I'm hoping that before I leave you can give me your autograph. My sister has threatened to kill me if I don't get it!"

"That's no problem. You can come over to the house with Brandon if you want."

"Oh, I would have liked to, but my dad has something planned for tonight. But I'll be glad to come over sometime, if it's fine with you. I want to be an actor and maybe you can tell me the best way to go about it."

"He's very good. He recently played Othello in our school play."

"The teachers at school say Brandon and I make

good best friends. We complement each other. He's all into the academics and I'm into the arts."

"That's only partially true," Brandon corrected. "You'd be brilliant at whatever you do. If you were taking the same courses as me, you'd be doing just as well in them. You just prefer the arts."

"You boys are going to keep my guests outside for the rest of the evening? He's here to visit me, so let him come in before I take a switch to each of your backsides." Mama grinned, contradicting the tone of her voice.

Dominic stepped forward, coming to a stop when he reached her. "So you going stand there after all these years and don't give me hug?"

Soon he was pulled into her arms. Even now she still smelled of baking. Back then she'd loved to bake. Of course, he and the other boys never complained. Every Sunday, he'd find himself at Mama's house. The delicious aroma of local pastries filled her home: sweetbread, turnovers and conkies, the same smells that presently greeted him as he released himself reluctantly from her arms.

"And this beautiful lady is your therapist? She's very beautiful. How old you are?" she asked.

"Twenty-eight."

"'Bout time you got married. Ain't anything wrong with marrying your therapist, especially if she's as beautiful as this one." She turned to Aaliyah and held out her hand, shaking Aaliyah's enthusiastically. "You're as beautiful as that grandson of mine says. I hope you taking good care of Dominic. As least he ain't walking with the cane I heard he'd been walking with. Means he's getting better."

Aaliyah blushed, looked flustered and then breathed in deeply.

"It's nice to meet you, too, Mrs. Johnson."

"In all my years the only person who called me Mrs. Johnson is the person who put this ring on my hand, and he's been gone for almost thirty years. You can call me Mama like everyone else."

Aaliyah nodded, not sure if she should speak.

"Good, and I'm going to call you Aaliyah. It's one those new fancy names, but at least I can pronounce it. And it's just like you, beautiful."

"You're a sweetheart," Aaliyah said.

"I've been told so, but be warned, I can be a battle ax, too, and this mouth here God give me to speak my mind, so I usually do just that. I've said many things before I think about what I said, but ain't no time I ever regret saying what I did."

She cackled, a deep-down-inside, hearty sound.

"Come, let's go inside. I been cooking and baking all day."

She led the way.

Dominic put the plate and spoon down and rubbed his stomach. He'd enjoyed the lunch of cou-cou and steamed flying fish, the island's national dish. He'd not eaten it in ages, but he remembered coming to this same home and feasting on the dish made of cornmeal swimming in a hefty amount of gravy.

"Dominic, I know you're probably readying to leave, but I wanted to talk to you before you go."

"That's fine."

"Aaliyah, I'll leave the boys to entertain you. I want to chat with Dominic about something private, if you don't mind."

"Of course not. I'm sure the boys will keep me occupied."

Mama rose from her chair and nodded to Dominic. He followed her out of the dining room and down the corridor to the sitting room. He waited until she was seated before he lowered himself onto the couch next to her.

"Your leg all right?"

"I'll be fine. It's been getting better each day."

"Your girl's doing a good job?"

"Yes, she's doing a good job."

"Good. I want you to be healthy."

He nodded, knowing that she had something more to say.

"I'm not sure exactly how to say this… I'm dying."

He turned to look at her. He didn't tell her that Brandon had told him. "How long do you have?"

"I'm not sure. The doctor says three months. Maybe six."

"Cancer?"

"Yes, I've been in remission for several years, but it's back."

"You don't have to worry. I'll take care of everything."

"Oh, I've already taken care of most things. It's Brandon I'm worried about."

"You don't have to ask. I'll take care of him."

"God bless you, son. I've been so worried thinking about what would happen to him. I'm his legal guardian, but I'm going to have to take care of making you that person."

"I'm fine with that. I want to do something for my best friend."

"I'm so sorry I have to do this to you. You just came back into our lives and I'm placing a burden on you. It's just that he has no one."

"It's fine. You don't have to worry about him. I'm glad I can do something to help. I could get my lawyer to take care of the papers. His office is in the city. I'll get him to come by on Monday."

"Okay. I haven't asked Brandon about any of this. I wanted to talk to you first. Didn't want to get his hopes up. But I'm sure it's not going to be a problem with him. He already idolizes you."

"He's my best friend's son. It's the least I can do. He's a good boy, so it's no burden."

"I know you want to do this for my son. But you still have to think about your future. Suppose you get married and your wife doesn't want a ready-made family?"

"I'm sure she will love him."

Mama cleared her throat. "So Brandon's assumptions were correct."

He didn't feel like beating around the bush. "You

mean his notion that I'm involved with Aaliyah. Yes, he was right."

"I could see it from the time I stepped outside and saw the way you look at each other." She laughed at her own skill of deduction. "You're in love with her."

He hesitated briefly. "I wish I knew what love was. Maybe if I'd ever been in love I would know. If it's the fast beating of my heart when she comes near, or the fact that I don't want to live another day without her, then it means I'm in love."

"You'll know when you are and you'll even know when it's time to let her know."

"Oh, I'm sure one day I'll be ready to let her know. At times, I feel so inadequate because of my hand and leg. Who'd want someone in this condition?"

"Condition! You're a good man. Yeah, you have a few minor problems with your hand and leg. And from what I can see right now, that leg is doing mighty fine."

"But I'm not sure if that's enough."

"For some other woman. I've only known Aaliyah for a few hours and already I'm so impressed I'd marry the two of you myself. But give it time. That's one of the problems with you young folk. Always in a hurry to do stuff instead of sitting back and looking at yourself in the mirror and finding out who you are."

"Interesting… That's all Aaliyah has been talking about recently. But I think I'm getting a better understanding of who and what I am. At least, much better than I understood two years ago. It's almost as if saving that girl and getting injured made me look at my life differently."

"That's good, son."

"Well, I should have said eventually. At first I was really angry at the world and God. Now I can see things differently." He paused. "You don't have anything to worry about. I'll take care of Brandon."

"Thank you," she said, tears glistening in her eyes. "I know you'll take good care of him."

"Thanks for having us over. I was wondering…we were wondering if Brandon could spend the night. We'll make sure he's back by tomorrow evening. I know he has school on Monday."

"Of course he can. And you can tell him what we decided."

"You want me to tell him?"

"He knows about my illness. But yes, I'd like you to tell him, so he knows that you want him. He's going to think I forced you into doing this because his father was your friend. He must know that you wanted him."

"Then I'll definitely do it."

"Come, I'm sure he's looking forward to spending the time with you and Aaliyah. He kept talking about his last visit."

"I'm going to also transfer his funds to you. The settlement for the accident by the insurance company was a lot of money. It will help when he is ready to go to college."

"That's no problem. I can take care of that."

"I know you will."

"Let's go. I am sure they are wondering what we could be talking about so long."

With that, she rose from the sofa and proceeded out of the room.

As she walked away, Dominic followed. For some reason, he felt happy. He'd done something that was important.

Of course, there was a bit of fear. He had no idea how to take care of a growing teenager and the thought scared him. What if he didn't do a good job?

By nine o'clock that night, Brandon was fast asleep. Even before the movie was midway done, he'd closed his eyes. They'd had a busy evening. Desmond had collected the pizza from Chefette Restaurant, a short distance away. The restaurant served the best pizza on the island.

While Aaliyah was accustomed to pizza with cheese and pepperoni, the islanders preferred their pizza with a lot more garnishes, and she could tell why. A thick chocolate milkshake had gone down well with the pizza. Of course, she could not believe that Dominic and Brandon had wolfed down so many slices. She'd eaten two of the ridiculously large slices and then had been full. But she had enjoyed the competition between the two males and had had no doubt that Brandon would be the eventual winner despite the valiant effort by Dominic.

"You need to take him up to his room, Dominic?"

"How am I going to do this, Aaliyah? I don't have

a clue what I'm doing. Maybe I should have told his grandmother I can't do it."

The look she gave him made him cringe, but when she spoke to him she spoke gently.

"I know you feel overwhelmed at the moment, but you're going to do fine."

With that he stood and walked over to Brandon, shaking him awake.

"Come and get to bed, Brandon. You've been sleeping here for hours."

At the boy's shocked look, he laughed. "Just kidding. You just missed half of the movie."

The boy jumped up and turned to Aaliyah. "Good night," he told her, a broad smile on his face.

"Good night. Have a good night's sleep."

"I'm sure I will. I'm tired."

She watched as they exited the room. She hoped it all worked out. Brandon needed a strong man in his life.

Dominic followed the teenager into the room. The boy no longer looked sleepy.

"Is it all right if I read for a while before I go to bed?" Brandon asked.

"Of course. You can read until you're sleepy again. You know where everything is. I'll see you for breakfast. Enjoy your sleep."

"I will, and thanks for having me over."

Dominic turned to walk away and then stopped. He turned back.

"I was going to talk to you about this in the morning." Brandon was already on the bed, a book in his hands.

The boy said nothing. A look of dread was on his face.

"Take that look off your face. I had a chat with your grandmother this evening and she told me about her illness."

Brandon nodded. Dominic could see the moisture in his eyes.

"How would you like to come live with me?"

"You mean here?"

"Yes, here. Wherever I am. Here or in the U.S."

"Now or after my…" Brandon couldn't say it.

"When it's time."

"Good. I want to be there for Mama."

"That's fine. Just wanted to know if it'll be okay with you."

"I hope my grandmother didn't force you to do this."

"She did ask me, but before I visited, I did think about it. After you told me about your dad's death, I thought about it, so your grandmother's request was only confirmation. You have no one after she is gone and while part of it is because your dad was my best friend, both Aaliyah and I think you are cool and like having you around."

Brandon smiled, his body relaxing as if a burden had been lifted off his shoulders.

And then he started to cry.

Dominic stared at him, not sure what to do, knowing that his own eyes had filled with tears.

He stepped over to the bed, sat down and placed his arms around the boy.

When Brandon had cried himself all out, he raised his head.

"I'm sorry. I didn't mean to cry."

"It's fine. You've lost your dad and now your grandma is ill. There is nothing wrong with crying."

"Men don't cry," he stated.

"That's not true. Let me tell you something. You are who you are. Don't let anyone dictate who you are. That's how people grieve and deal with death and their loved ones. If God didn't want you to cry, He would not have given you the capacity for the emotion."

"I never looked at it that way." He paused. "But don't expect me to cry too often."

"I look at it this way. When you need to cry you'll know. I won't think less of you if you ever cry."

Brandon nodded his head.

"Good night, sir. And thanks for everything you're doing for me."

"You have a good night. Everything is going to be fine."

The boy slipped between the covers and was soon fast asleep.

As Brandon lay there, Dominic realized how much he looked like his father.

He felt all choked up inside. He'd not cried for his friend and did nothing as the moisture trickled down his cheeks.

* * *

When Dominic entered the bedroom, Aaliyah looked up from the book she was reading. She could tell he'd been crying. She was glad. He'd needed to cry…for Adrian and Mama. She was sure there were more tears, but men with their macho attitudes never failed to amuse her.

She put the book down and held out her arms. He smiled and walked over to the bed. He needed comfort, and that's what she would offer him.

"Marry me," he said, when he was lying with his head against her chest.

While he'd taken a moment, she'd not expected that it would come to this.

"Are you sure?" she asked. "Are you absolutely sure?"

"Mama told me something today that I've been thinking about all evening. She said that when I'm in love, I'll know I'm in love. And that's it, simply said. I love you, Aaliyah, and I want to marry you. I want to spend the rest of my life with you."

She smiled, nodding her head. "Of course I'll marry you. I want to be in your life forever."

Epilogue

Aaliyah watched as her sisters and Cheryl cooed over the babies. She was an aunt. Her nieces, Gillian and Alana Grayson, were growing nicely and were adorable. Aaliyah had fallen in love with them that day at the hospital when "the aunts" had finally been allowed to see their nieces.

Today she was celebrating her three-month anniversary. She glanced down at the diamond ring on her hand. She couldn't believe she was married again.

She glanced across at Cindi. She'd grown to love her newfound sister as much as she loved Eboni. Cindi's personality hadn't changed much. She didn't talk much, didn't have time to spend on triviality, was focused on her work and didn't appear to have time for love. Even getting her to come to the monthly girls' night out was a challenge.

Aaliyah knew her sister enjoyed being with them, but she knew Cindi would much prefer to be at home planning her classes or working on her latest best-seller.

Keisha was another story. Their youngest sister had come home from Europe and the reunion had been an emotional one. But Aaliyah was worried about her youngest sister. Keisha had remained quiet and reserved, but Aaliyah had noticed a haunted look in her eyes when she thought no one was looking.

However, the reason for being here tonight was to tell them her good news. They all thought that they were at a routine girls' night out.

"Okay, ladies, I want to talk to you about something important."

"Can't you see we are playing with Gillian?" Cheryl chided.

"Yes, I can see, Cheryl. I think it's about time you marry one of the hunky men who always seem to be attached to your arms and get your own little bundle."

"Oh, girl, the temptation is there, but none of them qualify. I used to think that marrying for security would be enough, but yours and Eboni's marriages have made me think differently. Why shouldn't I wait for a man to fall deeply in love with? Hopefully he'll have a sexy body, a long tool and want to make love every night!"

"Cheryl, I'm going to bet you that some man is going to come along when you least expect it."

"Okay, I'm going to stop making fun of this institution you ladies hold so dear. I'm not holding out hope for me. I'm just very picky."

"Cheryl," Cindi chided, "I want to hear what Aaliyah has to say."

She hesitated briefly.

"I'm pregnant."

"Oh, my God, girl. Another one! What's wrong with you married women? Enjoy your honeymoon before you start putting buns in the oven."

"Well, it's what Dominic and I wanted. We didn't want to wait. Brandon is totally approving. He wants to be a big brother."

"How is he adjusting?"

"He's doing well now. Just went back into school, but he misses his grandmother. Heard him crying the night of the funeral, but Dominic was there for him. He'll be fine. We're just waiting for the adoption papers to be finalized."

"So when is the baby due?"

"It's just the beginning of the third month so we still have lots of time to go."

A wave of happiness washed over her. When her sisters and Cheryl all moved toward her, arms outstretched to offer hugs and kisses, she thanked God for giving her this life. For years she'd felt abandoned and lonely. He'd given her Andrew, who had come into her life and given her hope, which had been shattered. Now she remembered that day she'd seen Eboni leave the foster home, her face unsmiling.

Eboni's family had been good for her. She'd blossomed into a strong, confident woman. But she'd also make a great mother. Her stepdaughter Kenya adored her.

When she returned home, she planned on making love to her husband. He'd just returned from Los Angeles after auditioning for a role in an upcoming movie, something he'd only dreamed about.

She was definitely living her happily ever after.

Dominic heard the unlocking of the door. Aaliyah was back and his heart soared with the joy of seeing her. He'd missed her. She'd wanted to stay in New York to spend some time with her family and he'd been slightly relieved.

While he'd loved to have had her with him in Los Angeles, he'd been cautious about expecting to get the role. He'd wanted to prove that he could do it. And he had.

He couldn't wait to tell her he'd been offered the role of a lifetime, playing alongside his idol, Denzel Washington.

Aaliyah stepped into the bedroom and walked slowly over to the bed. She crawled onto the bed and straddled him, bending over to place a soft kiss on his lips. Immediately she felt the familiar charge of energy and wished she could strip her clothes right off and make love to him, but she knew he wanted to tell her his news.

"So are you going to make me wait all night?"

"I got it," he said without hesitation.

Her squeal of happiness reflected how he was feeling inside.

"Aaliyah, you don't want to wake Brandon. He'll think that something is wrong."

"At ten o'clock I'm sure he's still watching television or on his iPad reading a book."

"He probably is."

"But he's happy. I know he felt good when we told him about the baby. He's as excited as we are."

"So we have a few things to celebrate tonight. Want to go take a shower?"

She glanced down, noticing his arousal.

"You're sure you want to take a shower?"

"I could postpone it for an hour or two," he replied, his hand finding its way under her skirt. He pulled her panties off, his fingers slipping immediately inside her moist warmth.

"I can see you're ready for me."

"I'm always ready for you."

Without hesitation, he flipped her onto her back where she lay, her eyes smoldering with flames as she looked up at him wantonly.

He spread her legs and positioned himself between them. When he slipped inside her, he cried out with joy.

He paused for a moment. He loved this woman

with all his heart and soul. She'd touched his heart in a very special way. She'd healed him.

He smiled at her and whispered softly, "I love you."

She smiled in return, and then he gave in to his passion. Tonight he didn't plan on sleeping much. He had every intention of making love to his wife all night long.

* * * * *